Echo-Foxtrot

Clare Revell

Echo-Foxtrot

Cover Art by *Nicola Martinez*

Watershed Books, a division of Pelican Ventures, LLC
www.pelicanbookgroup.com PO Box 1738 *Aztec, NM * 87410

Watershed Books praise and splash logo is a trademark of Pelican Ventures, LLC

Publishing History
First Watershed Edition, 2015
Paperback Edition ISBN 978-1-61116-530-2
Electronic Edition ISBN 978-1-61116-529-6
Published in the United States of America

Dedication

For Luke, Callum, Jack, and Matt. The best nephews an
aunt could ask for.

Praise for
November-Charlie, *Book 1 of* Signal Me

"Three teens, a forty-foot boat, two oceans, and a mission: what could go wrong? Plenty! Clare Revell takes readers on an adventure of a lifetime as her young characters encounter one danger after another on their quest to rescue Mr. and Mrs. Kirk after authorities have given up the search." ~ Kathleen Friesen

"The incredibly talented Clare Revell has cooked up another amazing treat in this fast-paced and enthralling adventure. I fell in love with Lou, Jim, and Staci from the very start. Ms. Revell has an incredible knack for writing strong suspense, and this YA story is no exception." ~ Mary Manners

1

Jim Kirk leaned back in the seat of the USAF helicopter and glanced at his sister Staci, wanting to make sure she was all right. Sitting in the seat beside him, Ailsa Cudby slid her hand into his. He squeezed it tightly as he turned his gaze to the window. He didn't want either of the girls to see the tears in his eyes. He'd left his best friend Lou Benson behind, something he'd sworn he'd never do. She was like a sister to him, even if she didn't want to admit it.

They'd been through so much together the past few months. They were like the musketeers. All for one and one for all.

It should have been all of them who stayed, or none.

Below them he could see the vast swath of blue Pacific Ocean. Above them the huge rotor blades whirled and thudded. The helicopter banked a little to the left as it changed to a new course heading. He craned his neck but couldn't even see Agrihan as a tiny dot anymore. There was nothing below him but blue water.

"It'll be OK, Jim." Ailsa's quiet voice came over the headset he wore.

Jim shook his head. Things would never be OK again. He slowly reached up and turned on the microphone attached to his helmet. "How can it be

1

when we left Lou behind?" he asked.

He blinked hard. He'd never see her again.

He looked down again at the logbook on his lap. One of Lou's coded entries lay in front of him. She'd written it in mirror writing, so he couldn't read it— until an officer had lent him a mirror. He read it again.

I'm dying. Mafuso reckons there is nothing he can do. Not that he told me that. He insisted I was fine and healing nicely. I overheard the conversation with Amilek, and when I confronted him, he didn't deny it. The infection in my damaged leg is too deep. Fixing it is beyond his medical knowledge, and we'll never get rescued in time. I've always known I'd never recover from this. That's why I'm not leaving Agrihan. I'll go with the others to the base and then come back here to the village and spend my last few days on our island in the sun. It's for the best.

Jim, when you eventually read this, forgive me for the way I've been acting. I didn't want you to know, because I hate goodbyes. I love you, I always have. Ailsa is good for you. Be good to her. Tell Stace I love her too. Take care of her. And tell Mum…

Tell her I love her and I'm sorry.

Jim turned his face back to the window, his eyes stinging and his stomach tying itself in knots. This was *his* fault. He'd lost her, because of a stupid idea he'd had to pay her back for drawing sharks, dots, and other things all over the logbook. Because of him, she was dying, and he'd left her behind to die alone.

Lord, if I'd known, I'd never have left her. I shouldn't have done it. Forgive me…for I can't forgive myself for this.

One of the officers touched his arm. "I need you to talk to the doc flying out to the island. She needs to know about your friend's injury."

Guilt flooded him anew and he swallowed hard.

"OK."

A new voice rang in his ear. "Hi, I'm Dr. Andrews. Can you tell me what happened?"

"Lou got attacked by a shark in September. I did what I could, but I'm no medic, and we didn't have much on board the boat."

"Did you call for help?"

The spear of guilt dug deeper. "No, we couldn't. The radio was broken and the phone had gone overboard in an accident. We were too far from land, so..." He paused. That was a pretty feeble excuse. He should have done more. He *was* the adult, after all. Forcing his emotions down—after all, he was a man and men didn't have emotions—he gave the doctor all the information he could, along with what plants Ailsa and the village doctor, Mafuso, had used.

"But her leg smells again," he finished. "And according to what I've just read in the logbook, there was nothing more Mafuso could do. She's dying."

"We won't let that happen," Dr. Andrews said firmly. "I have the OR standing by and I'm taking a team with me. Colonel Fitzgerald is treating her now, and I'll start working on her as soon as I arrive."

"I don't know her blood type or her allergies. Nichola, her mum, would be the best person to ask. I know she, Lou, gets a lot of migraines."

"I've already spoken to Mrs. Benson."

"Is she really there?" he asked. "And my parents?" It wasn't that he doubted Colonel Fitzgerald's word that they were alive—after all, the officer had no reason to lie to them—he just wanted to be sure before he allowed himself to hope.

"They sure are, and planning on meeting the chopper as soon as it lands."

Jim closed his eyes as the doctor signed off and the headpiece went quiet. *Thank You, God, for keeping my parents safe. Let the medical team get to Lou in time. Let Colonel Fitzgerald persuade her to come back or have him bring her kicking and screaming, 'cause I can't lose her now. Not after all we've been through.*

Staci kicked him. "Hey, don't fall asleep. You're not allowed to fall asleep. We're going back to civilization and to find Mum and Dad."

He opened his eyes. "I'm not sleeping."

"And no checking your eyelids for holes either like Dad does on a Sunday afternoon. We all know what that means. It's like reading with your eyes shut."

"OK." Jim smiled slightly. Not even her enthusiasm would rub off on him at this point.

"You suppose Mum and Dad will be cross we left on our own?"

"They're bound to be. Ground us for at least fifty years, most likely."

Staci scrunched up her nose for an instant, then grinned. "Sounds good to me. I don't want to leave a nice, warm house with glass windows and a roof that doesn't leak for a long time. Just think, Jim. A house that has light switches. Hot water that comes from a tap and plenty of it. Bubble bath. Sheets. Blankets. Proper toilets that flush, with a lock on the door, and toilet paper. Meals I don't have to cook. Roast chicken, chips, and pizza. And chocolate. They can ground me as long as they want. Sounds like heaven to me."

"Nothing like heaven," Ailsa said. "And that's you sorted. Me, on the other hand?"

Jim shook his head. "She'll be bored within a week. And begging to be allowed out or to watch TV or something. Mum's idea of grounding us is no TV, no internet, no phone, and no going out unless we're escorted by her." He looked at Ailsa. "And you're staying with me."

She smiled. "If your parents want me."

"*I* want you," he said. "Forget the fact you have nowhere else to go. Besides, we're both over eighteen, so we're adults now. We can do what we want. Well, within reason, as it has to be legal." He paused, running his fingers over the back of her hand. "And most important of all? I love you."

"Love you, too."

"Good. So don't give me any of this leaving-me rubbish. I want you to stay."

Staci rolled her eyes. "Oh, please, if you're going to get soppy and kiss her, then go find a room. Oh wait, you can't." She put her hands over her eyes. "Go on then. You got ten seconds before I look. Jim and Ailsa sitting in a chopper..."

Jim grinned and kissed Ailsa's cheek. "I mean it. I want you to stay with us."

She smiled. "I'd like that too. OK, Stace, you can look now."

Staci peeked between her fingers. "Are you sure? I'm way too young for that kind of thing."

Jim snorted. "Yeah, right. And what was the name of that boy band again?" He winked. "You know, the one in the poster in your room where you'd stand on tiptoes on the bed and kiss each of them good night..." He broke off laughing as she kicked him.

"Insult me all you want. I don't care." She grinned at him. "We're going home..."

2

Lou Benson stood motionless on the beach of Agrihan as the helicopter vanished into the cloudless blue sky. At least Jim, Staci, and Ailsa were safe. Something they hadn't been since they got shipwrecked here back in November, two months ago—although technically, they hadn't been safe since embarking on this trip back in June.

Her leg throbbed and she shivered.

She cast a sideways glance at the tall man with salt-and-pepper hair standing beside her in his green flight suit. "Are you still here? You should have gone with them, Jack."

"Why?" Her would-be rescuer, Colonel Jack Fitzgerald, United States Air Force, moved to stand in front of her, hands on hips, his piercing brown eyes boring into her.

She wished he'd just go away and let her die in peace. She was hot, cold, couldn't stop shaking, and knew from the smell that the infection in her leg was raging uncontrolled throughout her body. The fact the pain had been reduced to a dull ache was another sign the end was near.

She accepted her fate. Death was no more than she deserved. She'd go back up the cliff path to where she buried Deefer and lie down on the ground there with him and sleep. They'd left home together and now they'd stay together on Agrihan forever.

"Why should I have left you here alone?" Jack repeated.

"Because you should have. You're ruining everything by staying." She headed across the sand, leaning heavily on her homemade crutches. Her ankle twisted beneath her and she fell, crying out in pain.

"Ruining what?" Strong hands gripped her and picked her up, holding her firmly in his arms.

She struggled, blinking away the tears of pain. "Leave me alone."

"You know I can't do that. Now do I carry you or can I trust you not to run off again?"

"How can I run when I can't even walk?" She could hear herself biting his head off and she couldn't stop it.

"So let's go back to the base and wait for the chopper. They're sending out another one to pick us up."

"Why?"

"Because I was sent here to rescue you, so that's what I'm going to do. It's called following orders. Besides, I made a promise to your mom not to come home without you."

"Fine." Lou closed her eyes and let him carry her. For an instant she felt safe, but the feeling didn't last long.

Jack carried her back up the beach to the base. He laid her down on the runway. "Right. You stay here while I get this fire going again."

"Not going anywhere. You didn't bring my crutches, but it doesn't matter. Nice to sit down for a bit." Lou pushed herself upright, shifting back against one of the crates Jim had found. She shut her eyes, shivering as she wrapped her arms tightly around her middle. She listened as Jack's running steps moved around the runway. Things had gotten so messed up, and she didn't know why.

Jim would say it was her lack of faith, but that was Jim.

She didn't need a God who let bad things happen to good people running her life for her. She was quite capable of running it herself. And if she then trashed it, well, then she had no one to blame but herself.

"Not sleeping, are you?" Jack's voice cut through her thoughts.

She forced open her eyes. "No, I'm not."

"Good. I don't want you to sleep yet." Jack draped the blanket he'd found around her shoulders.

"Why not?"

"It's not bedtime yet. When did you last eat or drink?"

Lou thought for a moment. "Yesterday morning-ish. But that was only water. I haven't had anything that isn't water for weeks. There is a distinct tea and coffee shortage here."

Jack sat beside her, pulling his knees up and resting his wrists on them. "You know, Lou, Nicky…" He paused. "Your mom says I'm like a bear with a sore head without at least three cups of coffee in the morning."

"Mum?" She tilted her head, confused. Mum's name was Nichola, not Nicky. Only Bill and Di called her Nicky. And anyway, she was thousands of miles away. "You know Mum?"

"Yeah, I do. You're pretty, just like she is."

"I'm not pretty," she retorted, pushing the blanket to the ground. "I'm ugly and crippled. And I have a tendency to kill those who get close to me. Or at least hurt them badly. They'll be better off without me."

"I'm sure they don't think so."

Lou shivered. "They will do. It's my fault. All of it."

He wrapped the blanket around her again. "Why's that?"

Lou took a deep breath and looked away. "We went fishing because I drew sharks and stuff all over the logbook. And I saw that Jim was asleep when the autopilot was off. He'd only dozed off for a minute or so, but I could have called or shaken his arm to wake up, but I didn't and the boat sank..."

She shifted a little, trying to get her leg in a position where it didn't ache quite so much. "Deefer dying was my fault too. I knew I should stay on the path, but I saw something and I went to investigate. I was about to step forwards. Deefer rushed me and knocked me over. He ran straight into one of those wild-animal traps the natives use. The trap sprung upwards, the metal teeth dug into him. I couldn't get him out."

Lou held her hands out in front of her. "I had his blood on my hands. I killed him. If I had stayed on the path, he would still be alive. When I went fishing with Jim, we went to get fish 'cause Jim was tired of not having fresh food. He'd done nothing but mention sharks for days. Didn't matter where we were, he saw sharks. In the Atlantic, Caribbean, and so on. We thought it was an excuse to stop us swimming. I was splashing in the water to annoy Jim. I attracted it. Then I tried to save the catch. If I'd left it, then I could have swum faster."

Tears blurred her vision and her voice wavered. "I can't go home. I'm dying. Mafuso said so. The others don't need to watch that. And it's not fair on Mum after I've been gone for so long."

Jack tossed more wood onto the fire. "Who's Mafuso?"

"We stayed in his village after the fire at Christmas. Think that was started by the volcano. Did you know it erupted? Got photos—it was pretty. Mafuso's a good guy. He's the village medic, trained by missionaries apparently. There was nothing he could do to halt the infection. Don't have long. Couple days maybe." She shrugged. "But it's OK. I can stay here with Deefer."

Jack put his hand over hers. "You'll be fine once we get you back to base."

She frowned. *Which part of dying didn't he understand?* "Go talk to Mafuso if you don't believe me. He's a week's walk in that direction." She pointed to the gate.

"Your mom loves you very much. She wants you back home."

She couldn't keep up with the way he kept changing the subject. "No, she doesn't."

"I know for a fact she does. After I met you in Cornwall, I contacted her. I saw you in the paper and realized you had run away."

"We didn't *run* away," she corrected. "Staci and I *stowed* away. It's different. We hid on the boat until Jim had left and it was too late for him to do anything about it."

"Stowed away or ran away, it's the same thing. But I never imagined you'd be silly enough to risk the Atlantic during the hurricane season."

Lou shrugged. "Didn't have a choice. They'd stopped looking for Bill and Di, so we went to look instead."

"When the wreckage of your boat was found, your mom was frantic. We've been looking for you for weeks. Your mom has been staying at my place since before Christmas."

"Mum's here?"

"She's waiting at the base. As are Jim and Staci's parents."

Lou looked at him for the first time since she'd begun speaking. "They're alive?"

"Yes, they are and all three of them are worried sick about you kids," he said. "They love you and just want you home safely. It doesn't matter what you've done or think you've done. No one is beyond help, and that includes you."

Lou shivered, tugging the blanket closer. Why was it so cold all of a sudden? "I told you, it's too late. Can I go sit with Deefer now?"

"In a few minutes. You don't look so good."

"Don't feel so good." She lay down on the tarmac and closed her eyes. Maybe she'd sleep for a minute and then go up the path.

"I'm going to set up an IV," he said. "Get some fluids into you."

"OK," she whispered. Nothing really mattered anymore.

Jack worked quickly and she barely felt the needle going into the back of her hand. "All done," he said. "The chopper will be here in about twenty minutes. There's a surgical team standing by at the base back home. They'll fix your leg, and we'll get you well again."

"Not possible," she murmured. "Just tell Mum I'm sorry and I love her."

"You can tell her yourself, kid." He pushed her hair back from her face. His touch was strangely comforting. Like her father's had been a long time ago. "You'll see her in a little while."

"Can I sleep now?"

"Not yet. I'm not going anywhere, OK?"

She nodded. Least this way, she wasn't alone. Because, although she'd gotten used to the idea of dying, suddenly the whole concept scared her.

3

Anderson Air Force Base grew underneath them.

Jim's stomach twisted. He wanted to see his parents desperately, but at the same time he didn't. He knew he was going to be in trouble for leaving in the first place, never mind for not having enough faith in the authorities, and God, to look after his parents and care for them and find them. And then there was taking Staci with him and willingly putting her life in danger.

Ailsa squeezed his hand. "It'll be OK," she said. "They love you."

He turned in his seat to look at her. "How did you know what I was thinking?"

"I know you. It hasn't been long, but I know the way you think. Remember my parents were missionaries, too. For some reason they, like pastors, expect way more from their kids than any other parents seem to do." She smiled at him. "Yes, they'll be mad, but they love you."

Staci bounced in her seat. For the first time in months, he could see the thirteen-year-old that she once was, shining through again. "We're here. Look, Jim—cars, planes, proper buildings..."

Jim nodded. "Yeah."

The helicopter circled and landed. Five airmen ran over to it, along with a medical team and three civilians.

His parents, Bill and Di Kirk, and Lou's mum, Nichola Benson.

Staci screamed, jumping up and down in sheer joy. "Look, look, look!"

"Mum and Dad," Jim said. His heart leapt into his throat. "They're really here."

Staci leapt out as soon as the door opened, still screaming and crying. "Mummy! Daddy!" She hugged both her parents tightly.

Jim sat still for a moment longer and then jumped out of the chopper, straight into the arms of his parents. He hugged them tightly, tears filling his eyes and unashamedly running down his face. "I thought you were dead..."

"We thought the same of you two," Dad said, pulling Staci into the group hug. "Running away was an incredibly stupid and thoughtless thing to do. Why did you do it? Why not let the authorities do their job?"

"I'm sorry." Jim took a deep breath. "You were missing. No one was doing anything, so I thought I'd find you myself. Then the girls stowed away and..."

"Don't get mad at Jim or Lou," Staci interrupted. "I wasn't going to be left behind."

"We were worried sick," Mum told them, her voice wobbling. "When we finally found a working telephone, Nicky told us you were missing—"

His mother took a deep breath. "We've been frantic, wondering where you were. Jack kept in contact, told us he'd found you, but..." She paused. "I am so mad at you."

"Guess we're grounded," Jim said quietly.

"For the rest of your lives," Dad said. "And then some. You of all people should know better, James."

Jim shifted. "Sorry."

Dad nodded. "We'll discuss this later."

Jim turned and looked for Ailsa. She was standing on the edge of the group, looking awkward. He grabbed her hand and pulled her close. "This is Ailsa. She's a missionary kid, too," he said. "She saved our lives several times."

Mum smiled. "Nice to meet you, Ailsa."

Staci grinned. "He forgot to mention she's his girlfriend."

Jim elbowed her. "Shh."

Ailsa blushed as she shook their hands. "Jim has told me so much about you."

Mum smiled. "I'm looking forward to learning about you."

Jim looked at Nichola. "I'm sorry."

Nichola hugged them. "I thought I'd never see you again," she said. She looked past them. "Where's Lou? Didn't she come back with you?"

The blonde officer looked at her. "Jack stayed behind with her, Mrs. Benson. He said to tell you he'll be back on the next chopper."

Nichola looked at her and then back at Jim. "Why didn't she come?"

"She's sick and not thinking straight." He sucked in a deep breath. "Deefer died a couple of days ago and what with her leg being infected again and all..."

"Her leg?" Nichola frowned. "How did her leg get infected?"

"She got attacked by a shark and..." He broke off as Nichola paled.

Dad wrapped an arm around her to keep her from falling. "Shark?" he asked.

Jim felt sick. How could his dad always make him feel so guilty with so few words? "We went fishing in

September. This shark attacked the dingy and sunk it, and she didn't swim fast enough. I did what I could, but I'm no doctor and we couldn't call for help, as we'd lost the radio and the phone and..."

He broke off. He could feel the anger and disappointment in all the adults and knew it was aimed solely at him. "I'm sorry..."

"September?" Nichola whispered. "But it's January now. That's four months..."

"It's my fault," Jim said. "The logbook will prove that. If she dies, I'll never be able to forgive myself and I don't expect you to forgive me either."

Major Corrigan looked at him. "There's a doctor on the flight going out there now. And Colonel Fitzgerald has basic medical training. She's in good hands."

"I don't understand," Nichola said.

"It's a life flight," the officer told her. "They can start treating her as soon as they land."

A dark-haired woman in a blue uniform with lots of ribbons moved over to them. "I'm General Kaylana Merrick, the commanding officer of Anderson AFB. Welcome to Guam."

Jim shook the offered hand. "Thank you. I'm Jim Kirk. This is my sister, Staci, and my friend Ailsa Cudby. We found Ailsa on Agrihan. Her parents were missionaries who died there several years ago in a plane crash, and she's been living on the island ever since. She saved our lives and came with us."

"The other chopper should be arriving on Agrihan any time now. The last report from Colonel Fitzgerald said that Miss Benson is with him and in a stable condition. This is Airman Trant, one of our medics. He'll take you to the infirmary to check you over and then we'll get you settled. You can have a bath, a hot meal, and so on."

Staci grinned. "A hot bath sounds wonderful. I haven't had one of those in forever. Or a hot meal that wasn't fish or fruit or some kind of weird vegetable. Don't suppose you have chips, do you?"

Dad shook his head. "If you ask for chips, you'll get given crisps. You have to ask for fries."

Staci frowned. "But I thought the Americans spoke English."

Dad took hold of her hand. "Not our English. It's a whole different language."

Jim slid his hand into his mother's, content to let someone else take charge and be the grown-up again.

"Let's get you all inside," General Merrick said. "And I'll check on the status of the other chopper."

****

Lou pulled the blanket tightly around her shoulders and shivered. The sun still blazed down, so why did she feel like she lay curled up in a freezer?

"Are you OK?" Jack asked.

"Cold."

Jack put a hand on her forehead. "You're hot. Humor me and let me take your temperature."

"Fine." She sighed. "You sure you're not my mother?"

"Quite sure. Your mom's a whole lot prettier than I am. Hold still a sec." Jack used one of the in-the-ear thermometers she hated. "It's 102 degrees. We need to get you cooled down some."

He rummaged around in the bag beside her and pulled out a vial and stuck in a needle. Next, he injected something into the line in her hand.

"There you go. That should help the fever."

Lou shook her head. "Go away, Jim. I'm tired. It can't be 2 AM already."

"I'm not Jim."

Lou looked at him blankly. "Bill? I'm sorry. I never meant to get Jim and Staci in trouble. It's my fault. Jim wanted to find you, and Staci and I ran away to go with him." She shivered, seeing Deefer sitting beside her. "I'll take you for a walk in a bit, boy. I'm really tired and don't feel so good. Should never have gone fishing and been shark bait."

"Shark bait?"

Lou did a double take, not sure why the dog was talking to her, but answered him anyway. "Jim was cross because I drew all over his precious logbook, so he fed me to the sharks…"

Deefer's radio crackled. The fact the dog was now wearing green uniform didn't strike her as strange either.

"Colonel, this is Dr. Andrews. Do you copy?"

Deefer snatched his radio. Why did his paw have fingers? "Hi, Doc. Where are you?"

"Five minutes away. How is she?"

"Pretty sick. Her temp is 102, resps shallow, pulse too fast for me to count, and she's talking to people who aren't here. Her leg is way worse than the kid's radio message said. It's very infected—my guess from the smell would be gangrene. I've started the IV to get some fluids into her. I've also given her paracetamol to reduce her temperature."

Lou squinted at him before her heavy eyes slid shut. "Deefer, I am here, you know. An' since when did you talk with an American accent?"

"Hang in there, Colonel. We won't be long. Out."

Jack shook Lou slightly. "Did you hear that?"

"Yes." Lou opened her eyes. "Jack? What are you doing here?"

"Rescuing a damsel in distress." He smiled. "Chopper's coming. We'll soon have you home safely."

"No..." She broke off and closed her eyes.

Jack's fingers touched her wrist. "Don't you dare die on me now, kid."

She forced her eyes open. "Not...going...to. Just wanna sleep..."

"In a bit. Look, here come the cavalry."

The chopper flew overhead and landed. A woman in a flight suit ran over to them before the dust settled. "Colonel?"

Jack smiled. "Hey, Doc. This is Lou Benson."

Dr. Andrews smiled. "Hi, Lou. I'm Doc Andrews. Anderson's CMO. Can I have a look at your leg?"

Lou nodded slowly, struggling to stay awake. "Tired, sleep now."

"Stay with us, honey," Jack told her. "You can sleep in a few."

Dr. Andrews pulled a face as she gently examined Lou's leg. "Does that hurt?"

"Not really. Not as much as it used to," Lou whispered. "Got bit by a shark..."

"I spoke to Jim and he filled me in."

"OK."

She and the medics lifted Lou onto the stretcher and strapped her on securely. Then they slotted it into the chopper. "I'm going to give you something to help you with the pain, Lou. You'll get sleepy too, but that way, you'll be more comfortable on the way back." She smiled. "And yes, you can sleep now."

Lou nodded. "Stay with me, Jack."

Jack sat next to her and took her hand. "I'm right here, kid. Your mom would have my guts for garters—her expression, not mine—if I let anything happen to you now."

"Mum's here?"

"Waiting for me to take you home."

Lou's eyes fluttered as the meds filled her system. "Tell her...sorry."

"You can tell her yourself, kid..." His voice faded as everything began to float.

4

Jim, Ailsa, and Staci tucked into the third plate of meatloaf, beans, and mash with as much enthusiasm as they had the first. Mum, Dad, and Nichola sat with them. His parents had eaten one plateful, although Nichola hadn't even gotten food. Three armed security officers sat at the next table.

Jim pushed his plate back. "That was wonderful," he said. "I'm nicely stuffed."

"It has been so long since I had what Mum'd term proper food," Ailsa said.

"It must be harder for you," Staci said. "After all that happened on the island with your parents and all."

"To be honest, it's not hard at all. Mum and Dad were never there, not in that sense anyway. It was just me. That part of my life is over. I shan't forget, but it is time to move on."

Dad looked over at her. "Ailsa, do you have any family at all I can contact for you?"

Ailsa shook her head. "No. It was just my parents and me. I never knew my grandparents and there aren't any aunts or uncles."

"What will you do?" Staci asked.

"I don't know. I never really thought beyond this point. I know Jim said he wants me around, but I don't want to get in the way."

"You're not in the way," Jim said quickly. "You

won't ever be. I want you with me, one way or the other."

"You'll stay with us," Mum said decisively. "If you want to, that is. Things have changed. Losing people you love puts things into perspective. We saw a lot of people lose family and everything they own in the last few months and we thought we'd lost Jim and Staci. I don't intend to lose any of you again. And if you have nowhere to go, then you can have a home with us."

"Thank you. I'd like that."

Mum nodded. "Good. At least until you get settled and decide what you want to do, if not longer."

Airman Trant appeared at the table. "I've come to take you three to the infirmary. The doc wants you where she can keep an eye on you for a few nights."

General Merrick came across, a look of concern on her face. "Mrs. Benson? The helicopter carrying your daughter is on approach. The doc asked me to prepare you as to Lou's condition."

Nichola looked up. "I thought they said she was stable?"

"Things are worse than we first thought. Lou is seriously ill. The doc is concerned about the massive infection in her leg. They had to do CPR at least once."

Nichola paled and sank back in her chair. "No," she gasped.

General Merrick put a hand on Nichola's shoulder. "We will do all we can. I have the best surgeons in the Air Force here." A helicopter could be heard outside. "That's them. She needs to go straight to surgery. If you want to see her, it has to be now."

Jim got up. "Can I come too, please?"

Nichola nodded.

Dad stood. "I'll go with and catch up with you guys in the infirmary." He looked at his wife. "Make sure they don't get lost en route, Di."

Mum held his gaze. "I don't intend to let them out of my sight."

Jim ran with them to where the helicopter had just landed. They stood in the doorway and watched as a second medical team swooped on it and deftly put the stretcher onto the waiting trolley. They ran with it towards the building, Jack running with them.

As they drew level with General Merrick, she halted them.

Nichola gasped as she saw Lou lying motionless, tubes and wires everywhere. Her eyes moved downwards until she saw Lou's red and swollen leg. "Lou, what have you done, baby?"

"We'll do what we can," Dr. Andrews promised and they ran on towards the OR.

Jack slid a hand into Nichola's. "They'll take good care of her, Nicky."

"Is she OK?" she asked, her gaze lingering on the vanishing med team.

Jack shook his head. "She's pretty sick. But she's in good hands. I've been praying constantly the whole flight home. I know God heard me. He'll do what is best for her." He ran a finger down her cheek. "What about you, honey? Are *you* OK?"

"I'm fine." She rubbed a hand over her eyes.

"No, you're not." He pressed his lips to the top of her head. "C'mon, I got time for a coffee first before the debrief. Let me just dump the bag."

Nichola smiled at him. "You shouldn't talk about people like that. And you should at least shower and change first."

Jack grinned at her, then glanced at his crumpled and stained flight suit. "You're right. On both counts. Give me ten minutes. I'll meet you in the mess." He squeezed her hand briefly and headed off.

Jim looked down. He felt horrible, useless, and alone. This was his fault. Didn't matter how much he apologized, if she died, it'd be solely down to him.

Dad touched his shoulder. "Come on, son. Let's go and find the others. Mum and I need to talk to you and Staci."

Jim nodded. "OK." He walked slowly with his father, not looking forward to anything his parents had to say.

In the infirmary, Staci lay curled up on the bed. "Jim, where's Lou?"

Jim sat on the bed next to her. "They took her straight to surgery. They're really worried about her."

"Is she going to die?"

He pushed a hand through his hair. The length of it hadn't bothered him in weeks, but now it did. All he wanted was to cut it. Daft...his best friend was dying and all he could think about was his hair. "She could. It's all my fault. If I hadn't taken her fishing because I wanted the fish..."

"I asked for the fish in the first place."

Jim shook his head. "It was my decision to take her fishing that morning, because I was angry with her. I wanted the fish more than anyone, because I was tired of tinned food. I should never have let you come. Either of you. I should have turned around soon as I found you both that first morning, never mind after her idiot stunt in the docks."

Dad slammed his hand down on the bedside unit. "James Tiberius Kirk. That's enough," he thundered. "I don't want a pity party or a let's-blame-each-other-or-myself attitude. James, I want you to explain, from the beginning. And I want all of it."

Jim shifted uncomfortably. "Where's the bag? It has the logbook in it…"

"Never mind the logbook. There's plenty of time for me to read that later. Just talk."

He glanced at the others and began from the beginning, explaining what he and the others had done. Explaining it all, the explosion in the docks, Hurricane Erika, the shark attack, the shipwreck, volcano, and forest fire made it sound awful. Which it was. And a miracle they had all survived.

He supposed it was a good job that God was looking out for them, because he hadn't done a very good job at all. And he was meant to have been the grown-up in all this.

"I'm so sorry. I just wanted to find you," he finished. "No one was looking and you'd been declared missing."

Dad nodded. "There wasn't any communication possible for days. Nothing much in or out where we were. There was a lot of damage, but we were high enough to avoid the floodwaters. It just cut us off. They managed to get the news crews into the main towns, but anything else just wasn't possible. It was chaos, no one knew where anyone was, so many people hurt, dead, or simply missing."

Mum took his hand. "We finally got rescued three weeks later and rang home. Nicky said you'd all left. We got the first flight home we could — which wasn't until September. By which point Jack had been in touch, saying he'd seen you all."

Staci looked up slowly. "Are we grounded?"

"Forever," Mum replied.

"Already asked that," Jim muttered.

"And got the same response," Dad said.

Jack came in. "Nicky's sleeping in my quarters here on base tonight in case Lou needs her." He held out his car keys. "I'm going to stay here as well so she's not on her own. You guys can drive yourselves back to the house when you're ready."

Dad took the keys. "Thanks, Jack."

Jim looked at Jack. "Any news on Lou?"

He shook his head. "She's still in surgery and probably will be most of the night. I'll see you in the morning."

Jim watched him leave. Salt burned his eyes. If Lou died, it would be his fault. How would he ever forgive himself? How would anyone else forgive him?

God, please, he began and broke off. He didn't know how to phrase it, but then it didn't matter, as God knew his deepest desires better than he did.

5

Beeping and hissing surrounded her. For a moment Lou thought she was in some kind of weird poacher trap. Not just one with vicious teeth, but hundreds of snakes that bit and stung. Voices echoed around her, snippets of conversation creeping into her mind as faces came and went.

"How is she, Doc?" That sounded like Jack.

"Colonel, are you still up? It's 0330."

"Heading to bed now. I promised Nicky I'd check in first."

"It's not good. We couldn't save her leg below the knee and the infection appears to have spread. We're pumping her full of antibiotics in an attempt to save the rest of her leg."

"Is she going to die? And don't sugarcoat it either. I need to be able to prepare Nicky for the worst."

"It's possible, yeah. She crashed again about half an hour ago. Each time that happens, it makes getting her back more difficult."

Everything faded again for a long time. Then more voices. "OK, we got her back."

"I want to see her…" That sounded like Mum, but she was in England.

"Not now, Nicky…"

"Yes, now." Footsteps echoed, mixing with the snakes and the beeps. "What happened?"

"She coded. We got her back this time. We'll watch

her carefully the next few hours."

"Coded? What does that mean? I don't understand...Jack?"

"Her heart stopped for a minute. But the doc got it started again. She's got a long road ahead of her still. She's very, very sick, Nicky. The doc doesn't know if she'll survive."

"This isn't fair—she's only sixteen. She can't die. I can't get her back only to lose her." Someone brushed something across her face. "Lou? It's OK. I'm here now. I'm not going anywhere. I need you, Lou. Don't leave me on my own. I can't do this, Jack. It feels like I'm saying goodbye."

****

Just after first light, Jim watched Jack leave the room at the end of the infirmary and glanced at Staci and Ailsa. They'd all been awake most of the night and now sat huddled on the one bed, waiting for news of Lou, which never came. "Jack, have you got a minute?" he called.

Jack smiled and walked across the room. "Hi. How are you guys doing? You're all up rather early."

"We're worried about Lou. Where is she? They didn't bring her in last night."

"They put her in intensive care. She's pretty sick."

Staci gripped Jim's hand tightly. "How sick?"

"She stopped breathing in the OR," Jack told them gently. "At the moment she is hooked up to machines that are breathing for her."

Ailsa asked, "What about her leg?"

"The docs couldn't save it because the damage and infection was too great."

"What did they do?" Jim asked, afraid of the answer.

"They amputated it."

"Amputate?" Staci asked, not familiar with the term.

"Cut it off," Jack explained. "From here." He pointed to just above his knee.

Jim thumped the bed in frustration. "I should have turned back and made for land when it happened," he said angrily. "I woke her up. I insisted she came with me, to pay her back for defacing the logbook. It's all my fault. And we still could have reached help months ago if I hadn't of wrecked the boat."

"Enough already. Lou doesn't blame any of you. She blames herself. She told me that whilst we waited for the chopper to come back for us."

"Will she be OK?" Ailsa asked.

"It's too early to tell."

A man walked in and Jack smiled.

"Ed. Buddy. How are you?" The two men exchanged a bear hug. Jack thumped the other man on the back.

A big, imposing figure dressed in blue, he replied in a voice that matched his stature. "Fine. You?"

"Yeah. Great. Good vacation? How're Cathy and the baby?"

"Doing great, and I'd hardly call paternity leave a vacation. No sleep, endless diapers, constant feeds. The baby's wonderful, but then it's early days."

Jack turned back to the others. "This is Sergeant Ed Peterson. He's been assigned to you while you are here. He'll escort you everywhere and answer any questions you may have and so on. He's one of the best. This is Jim, Staci, and Ailsa. OK, guys, I got to go do some work. Be good."

"This can't be happening," Staci said after Jack left. "I'm asleep and I shall wake up on the island in a minute."

"Oh, it's real, kiddo."

"Lou has to be OK. She has to be."

Sergeant Peterson came over with a pile of clothes. He put them on the bed and handed them some each. "Nothing fancy and I had to guess at some of the sizes, but they should fit. Once you are dressed, you can go for breakfast. Your parents will be in a little later."

Staci stood up. "Where's the bathroom?" she asked. Ailsa grabbed her clothes and followed as Sergeant Peterson led the way down the corridor.

Jim wandered across to the line of windows, curious as to what was there. Apparently the intensive-care unit was just across the hallway. It made sense having it relatively close to the nurses' station.

He could see Lou lying on the bed and felt guilty. She faced the rest of her life crippled because of him. Even though Jack said he wasn't to blame, he still felt guilty. Airman Trant stood next to him, writing on a clipboard. "Is she really as sick as Colonel Fitzgerald said?"

Trant nodded. "The machines are keeping her alive."

"She won't thank you. She wanted to die before they took her leg, so she definitely won't want to live now."

"We have trained counselors she can talk to."

"She won't want to do that either. She can be a stubborn thing at times. Can I see her?"

"Tomorrow. We need to run some more tests on you first. Check you for parasites and things like that."

Great. "Seriously?" Jim rolled his eyes. "You gonna check for nits as well?"

Airman Trant nodded. "You could have brought anything back with you. It's standard procedure everyone goes through on returning to base."

"Yeah, well, they can cut my hair while they're at it," Jim muttered. "I look like a girl."

Staci laughed from behind him. "You look more like a rock star minus the tattoos," she chuckled. "Though if you want to annoy Mum and Dad more, go for it."

Breakfast was a feast as far as they were concerned, with as much as they could eat or drink and then some. Ailsa drank so much coffee that Staci told her she would drown, or at least float all day, but they all avoided the cold tea in the dispenser. Finally, even Staci was full and pushed her plate away.

Sergeant Peterson folded his serviette. "The general has asked to see you three when you finished here."

Jim felt his stomach sink and threaten to eject what he'd just eaten. He was going to be arrested, he just knew it.

Staci pulled a face. "It's like being dragged before the headmaster at school. Even if you've done nothing wrong, you still feel guilty."

"But we have done something wrong," Jim reminded her. "We left home. Because of that Deefer is dead and Lou is dying."

"But if we hadn't left England, we would never have rescued Ailsa," Staci argued. "And you wouldn't be able to look all sappy eyed at each other the whole time."

When they reached the general's office, Sergeant

Peterson knocked and the door opened.

"In you go," he said. He shut the door behind them and stood guard outside.

"Sit down," General Merrick said. Her eyes were cold and her voice sharp.

Three chairs had been placed opposite her desk. They sat, all feeling slightly uncomfortable. "Thank you for sending the helicopter for us yesterday, General," Jim began.

"It arrived just in time from what Colonel Fitzgerald tells me," General Merrick said dryly. "It was sheer luck we picked up your signal. We don't use Morse code anymore, but I insist on all my airmen knowing it. A routine training session was running when you sent your first SOS. I sent the plane out in response to that. And again after your second message."

"Thank you."

General Merrick looked at them. "Ailsa, I understand that you'd been on the island for six years since a plane crash."

"Yes, ma'am. My parents were killed. A local tribe found me and cared for me. When the others came along, I joined up with them."

"Are there any relatives I could contact for you?"

"No, no one. It's just me now."

General Merrick smiled. "OK. What I have to say now doesn't apply to you. Sergeant Peterson will take you back to the infirmary. The doctors have a day of tests planned for you. I believe you asked about going off the base?"

Jim nodded. "If that's allowed."

"As soon as Dr. Andrews gives you the all clear, you may leave with your parents."

"Thank you." Ailsa squeezed Jim's hand as she got up and left the room.

General Merrick looked at Jim and Staci. "Do you have any idea what you have done?" she asked. "Hours of manpower spent both in Britain and around the world searching for you. Your parents and Mrs. Benson were worried sick about you. Running away solves nothing. It just gets you in more trouble than facing the issue in the first place."

"We didn't run away," Staci interrupted. "We were looking for Mum and Dad."

"*I* was looking for them," Jim corrected her. "You and Lou stowed away."

General Merrick silenced him with a look. "Mrs. Benson was devastated at the apparent loss of your parents. That, coupled with your disappearance, drove her to the edge of a nervous breakdown. Colonel Fitzgerald contacted her when he met Lou in Cornwall and then went back to bring you all home, only to find he'd missed you by a few minutes. He called her again on July 24, after he met you on Grand Turk. Then again on August 12, where at Mrs. Benson's request, he had paid for the boat repairs. He struck up a friendship with her and was largely responsible for helping her recover. Your parents arrived back in England, desperate to see you, only to hear you'd run away. And when a plane on a routine recon spotted the wreck of *Avon*, your parents and Mrs. Benson flew out here. They've been here ever since, worrying about you."

General Merrick looked hard at Jim. "As the eldest, you should have stopped this escapade from ever happening."

"It wasn't all Jim's fault. Lou and I had the idea of

stowing away and going with him," Staci said, not willing to let Jim cop all the blame. "I didn't want to go to boarding school. I didn't want to be separated from my brother. Jim kept us safe."

"Safe? From what I understand, you encountered a hurricane, a shark, you were shipwrecked, had a run-in with an erupting volcano, a forest fire, near starvation, not to mention the death of the dog. Need I go on?"

"You're right. I messed up. Big time," Jim whispered. "This whole thing is down to me. I was the responsible adult. I'm sorry. If I could take it all back, redo it all, I would." He looked down, wishing he could just vanish.

"A tiny pebble causes many ripples," General Merrick said. "There was one good thing to come out of all this though."

Jim looked up, his face burning. "I can't see any."

"That young woman you rescued, Ailsa. She may have stayed there for the rest of her life, if you hadn't come along when you did."

"What will happen now?" Staci asked. "Are we in trouble?"

"As far as I am concerned, I have spoken to you and will not be taking any further action. What your parents decide is another matter altogether. Once the medics here have discharged you, Colonel Fitzgerald has said you can stay with him until your parents return to England. Sergeant Peterson will accompany you at all times while you're on the base. I suggest you follow his instructions to the letter."

Jim inclined his head. "OK."

"OK, you may leave." General Merrick turned her attention to her paperwork.

Jim took the hint and led Staci from the room.

****

That afternoon, back in the infirmary, they endured a huge battery of tests. Staci complained loudly and vehemently, but to no avail. Sergeant Peterson stood watch the whole time from his spot by the door.

Staci looked across at him. "Don't you ever get bored standing there?" she said.

"Not with all the entertainment you're providing," he replied.

"Sorry?"

Sergeant Peterson raised an eyebrow. "Until you have been checked out thoroughly, you can't leave the base. You might be contagious. And the more you argue, the more tests the doc will do. Trust me. Jack and I have been there and tried it."

Jim looked up, wincing as they took yet more blood. At this rate he wouldn't have any left. "How long have you known Colonel Fitzgerald?"

"Since high school. We joined the Air Force together, served in several places together, best man at each other's weddings, and wound up here at the same time."

"So how come he's a colonel and you're only a sergeant?" Staci asked.

"Staci." Jim glared at her. "You don't ask questions like that."

Sergeant Peterson smiled. "That's OK, Jim. It's one of those things, I guess. He got one of his promotions in the field during the Gulf War."

Nichola came out of the ICU with Dad and Mum.

"Hi, guys. How are you doing?"

"Feel like a pincushion," Jim said.

"A starved pincushion," Staci added.

Jim rolled his eyes. "It's only been three hours since you ate last."

Nichola turned to Sergeant Peterson. "Hi, Ed." They hugged. "How are Cathy and that new baby of yours?"

"Both fine. We finally decided on a name. Deborah. You and Jack need to come visit. Cathy would love to see you."

Doc Andrews came over with a clipboard. "All done." She smiled. "I want you to sleep here again tonight. You are all in remarkable good health. Slightly under nourished, but otherwise OK. You can go and get some food and then a brief walk. You could go and visit the base hairdresser. I know how desperate Jim is for a haircut. Then back here."

Staci jumped up. "Yay. Food."

Jim looked at the doctor. "How's Lou doing?"

"She's doing OK," she said.

Jim read swiftly between the lines. "So why is she still unconscious?"

"She's still heavily sedated. She's got a long road ahead of her once we do wake her. She'll need to learn to walk again, for one thing."

"Did she really lose her leg?" Staci asked, taking hold of her mother's hand.

Dr. Andrews nodded. "Yes, she did. You did a really good job though, Jim."

"Not good enough," he muttered. "It got infected almost immediately, but I didn't have anything to treat it with. 'Cept prayer."

"Never underestimate the power of prayer," Dad

told him.

Dr. Andrews nodded again. "I've never known healing prayers to fail." She smiled and turned her attention to the clipboard. "Anyway, tomorrow morning you all have an appointment with the base counselor."

Staci shook her head. "No way."

"It's not an option. Afterwards, you can leave the base for a couple of hours."

Dad looked at his daughter. "Mum, Ed, and I will take you clothes shopping, but only if you cooperate with the counselor first."

Staci sighed. "Not that desperate for new clothes, but fine."

6

Once the counseling was done, Jim, Staci, and Ailsa, with the ever-present Sergeant Peterson, went to find Nichola. Jim tapped on the door of the ICU.

Nichola smiled and came to the door. "Nice haircut, Jim."

He ran his fingers through it. "Thank you. It's so nice not having it brushing my shoulders anymore. Staci doesn't like it, but it was this or a complete grade four, which would really have been one extreme to the other."

She nodded. "That would be too different even for you. How did the counseling go?"

Jim shrugged. "It went. How's Lou?"

"No change. Coming for some lunch? I need to talk to you all."

"Sure. After lunch Mum and Dad are taking us into town. The sergeant is coming too."

Nichola looked at Sergeant Peterson.

He smiled. "I have been instructed not to let them out of my sight. They will be quite safe."

Staci piped up. "Don't worry, Nichola. After yesterday we won't do anything stupid."

Nichola looked at her. "Oh?"

Staci explained. "General Merrick read us the riot act. We've been bound over to keep the peace. But you know, Dad was right, talking can be a good thing. All that talking has made me hungrier than ever." She headed off towards the door.

Jim shook his head. Nothing changed. Well, some things did.

One life was irrevocably changed because of a choice they made. Choices, consequences, and repercussions. Something he and Lou would live with for the rest of their lives.

They walked to the mess hall and collected their lunches. Sitting down at a table, they noticed that Peterson didn't sit with them this time.

Nichola looked at them across the table.

Jim sucked in a deep breath. "Before you say anything, I'm, that is, we're sorry. I know we hurt you and caused you to worry. What we did was wrong. It seemed the right, no, make that the only choice at the time, but it was anything but. It almost cost Lou her life. I guess it still might and I don't expect you to forgive me for that."

"I don't blame you, Jim. I should have been more considerate of your feelings instead of acting like nothing had happened. But the important thing is you're all here and safe, and so are your parents. For the time being, we'll all be living together at Jack's place."

Staci looked at her. "Mum and Dad as well?"

"Until they go back to England, yes." She looked at Ailsa. "And you can stay with us as long as you want."

"Thank you."

"How big is Jack's place?" Staci asked. "Is there going to be enough room for all of us? That's like eight of us."

"There are several bedrooms, plus a den, lounge, and a separate dining room. He'll fit everyone in, don't you worry about that."

"What about when we go back to England?" Jim said. "Mum and Dad sold our house before they left on the last trip. And your flat isn't big enough for all of us."

"I sold the flat a while ago. Your parents inherited Aunt Edith's house when she died in October, so you'll be living there." She broke off as Jack came into the mess with his flight team. He waved at her and she waved back. "So," she said. "I hear you lot are hitting the town this afternoon?"

Ailsa smiled. "Yeah. Clothes shopping and Jim needs to go to the bank."

Dad and Mum came in. "You guys ready to go?"

Jim smiled at them. He didn't want the 'novelty' of seeing his parents to ever wear off. "Yeah."

Nichola looked at him. "Did you keep a diary at all?"

"Yeah, we did. We wrote in the logbook several times a day. We all wrote in it." He paused. "It's not easy reading, especially some of the entries."

"May I read it? I need to know what happened to Lou."

"Sure. It's in the infirmary, I think. In a big waterproof bag, along with everything we managed to save from *Avon*. Not an awful lot, really. I'll go and get it." He stood up. "I won't be long." He stood, Sergeant Peterson rising to follow him.

Nichola got to her feet. "I'm going to sit with Lou, so I'll come with you."

In the infirmary, Nichola stopped by Dr. Andrews's office to speak with her. Jim opened the bag by his bed and removed the logbook. The folder looked battered and worn in the cold light of day and he hesitated showing it to anyone.

Sergeant Peterson took one look at it and fetched an arch-lever folder from a stationery cupboard. "Use this."

"Thank you."

He helped Jim transfer the logbook to the new folder.

Jim put the charts and official papers into the original folder, which he put back in the bag. He took out Lou's sewing. The frame was empty. He looked at it, wondering what she'd done with the piece that was on there, and then put it back. In the bottom of the bag, he found the piece he wanted. The completed, rolled-up piece labeled *For Mum*. "OK," he said. "I just want to see Lou for a minute."

Jim went into the intensive-care unit, while Sergeant Peterson watched through the window. The machines beeped and the ventilator hissed and hummed. "I'm sorry, Lou. Don't leave us. We have come too far together."

He sat next to her and held her hand. "You're cold. You missed out yesterday. We got yelled at for running away. Well, not yelled at exactly, because she didn't raise her voice once, but she made her point all right. It wasn't your mum or my parents either. We got hauled in to see General Merrick. You haven't met her yet, but she's the boss around here. I don't know if they've told you, but they couldn't save your leg. I think we both knew that was likely deep down though."

The figure on the bed didn't move.

He gripped her hand. "You have to fight this thing, Lou. Don't let it win. The people here are great. They have done all they can. They brought you back from the abyss. It's up to you now. It's not time for you to go. Not yet." There was a tap on the window. Jim turned and Sergeant Peterson beckoned him. Jim nodded. "I got to go. Mum, Dad, and our escort are taking us out for a bit. See you later." He left the logbook on the chair for Nichola and returned to the mess hall where the others were waiting impatiently.

"There you are. Thought you'd got lost," Staci said. She still had tight hold of her mother's hand.

"No chance of that." Jim grinned. He glanced up at his father as he dropped a hand on his shoulder. "I thought we could get this framed as well." He held out the fabric with its label. "Lou was adamant Nichola should have this piece when it was finished."

Dad smiled. "Good idea. Nicky would like that."

"Ready to go?" Sergeant Peterson asked.

"Sure."

****

Lou lay still, unable to move as pain filled the darkness surrounding her. She could hear voices again. They came and went, mostly ones she didn't recognize. Jack had been there a couple of times, and she thought she heard Jim at one point but wasn't sure.

There was someone crying. But it wasn't Staci. It sounded like her mother, but it couldn't be. She was thousands of miles away. Lou wanted to open her eyes and look, but they refused to cooperate and she remained a prisoner of the darkness.

There were more voices, then one that pierced the darkness with some clarity. Jack...

"Nicky, are you OK?" Sobs answered him before his voice came again. "Nicky, it's OK, honey. I'm here."

There was a pause before her mother's voice

answered. "I was reading their logbook and Jim's account of the shark attack. It's awful. They went through so much. I am so mad at her for running away, but so pleased she is back. I don't know whether to yell at her, ground her, or just hug her to bits. But then I'm terrified I'm going to lose her after all. There is so much I want to say to her…"

Something beeped, and then she was floating above the bed. That was weird. She could see Mum and Jack sitting by the bed and herself lying there—but she didn't look right. It seemed a piece of her was missing.

The scene unfolded below her, just like watching a movie, only she was the star without doing anything. Lou watched from the ceiling, not sure what was going on. She wished she could give Mum a hug, stop her from crying.

"Her blood pressure's dropped." As Jack rose out of his chair, the monitors flatlined and alarms began to blare. "Doc," he yelled. He put a hand on Lou's neck, then thumped on her chest and started CPR. "Told you the other day, kid, don't you die on me. Nicky, go and get the doc. Now."

Mum didn't move. "Help, someone," she screamed.

Dr. Andrews rushed across the room. She took the situation in at a glance and grabbed the crash trolley. "Colonel?" she asked.

"BP dropped, then she crashed." He stood back, letting the medics take over the CPR. He pulled Mum to one side, holding her gently.

Dr. Andrews took the scene in a practiced glance, her eyes resting on a drop of blood on the floor. She pulled back the sheets. The bottom one was heavily bloodstained.

Lou frowned. Where'd her leg go?

"I need her back in the OR, stat. Let's move, people."

Mum wrapped her arms tightly around her stomach. She was as white as a sheet. She got in the way as they moved Lou's bed. "What's wrong? Where are you taking her?"

Jack pulled her to one side. "She needs to go back to the OR. She's bleeding."

"I'm going to lose her, Jack."

"Not if we have anything to do with it. Let me make a phone call to see if I can take off the rest of the day. I'll be right back. Then you and I are going to go to the chapel to sit and pray while she's in surgery."

Everything floated, and Lou let the darkness take her.

****

Jim, Staci, and Ailsa stood on the street corner, Mum and Dad beside them, and Sergeant Peterson just behind. Traffic whizzed past them.

"It's so busy," Jim said.

"I'd forgotten what traffic was like. Haven't missed it though," Ailsa said. The lights changed and they crossed the road.

Sergeant Peterson took them to a craft store that had a framer.

Jim showed them Lou's picture and Staci and Ailsa chose a frame and mount for it.

"Two hours OK?" the girl asked.

"Sure. Do I pay now?"

"When you pick it up."

Dad looked at him. "I'll pay for it, James," he said. "And don't argue."

Jim nodded. "Sure, Dad. Thank you." He wasn't going to admit it, but it was nice not having to worry about little things like money anymore.

Next, they went clothes shopping and then ended up in a fast-food place. Jim savored every mouthful, whereas Staci, hungry as ever, scarfed hers down and wanted more.

Dad laughed. "That's the Staci I remember." He got up and took Staci to get another burger.

Jim looked at Ailsa. "I hate being escorted everywhere."

"You'd do the same in their place, Jim. You have to earn their trust again."

"I know." Jim reached across the table and took her hand. "Ailsa, I..." He broke off as Staci came back.

Ailsa smiled at him. "Later," she said.

"Later what?" Staci asked, her mouth full of burger.

"Don't talk with your mouth full," Mum chastised.

Staci rolled her eyes and chewed as quickly as she could, then swallowed. "Later what?" she repeated.

"She reckons she's going to beat me at Phase 10 tonight," Jim said.

"She's probably right. You're rubbish at it."

"Sounds like a challenge to me," Sergeant Peterson said. "Personally, I've never heard of it."

"It's a card game. We'll have to teach you," Jim said. "Sounds like I shall need all the allies I can get."

****

Jim, Staci, and Ailsa arrived back on the base

much later than they had planned. It was dark. Nichola stood in the door to the infirmary. She looked awful.

"Hi, Nichola. Can we see Lou?" Jim asked.

Nichola shook her head. "Dr. Andrews wants her left alone tonight. She didn't have a very good day."

Staci frowned. "Lou or the doctor?"

Jim shoved aside his disappointment. "Don't start, Stace. We can give her the picture tomorrow. It's not going anywhere."

Staci sulked anyway. "I want to see her."

"We all do," Jim said.

"You can see her in the morning," Dad said. "Now you guys go ahead with Ed and Mum. I want a few words with Nicky, then I'll catch you up."

7

After the lights were dimmed that night, Jim lay awake. He looked at the clock on the wall—almost eleven. Perfect. He sat up and looked at the others. Both Staci and Ailsa were fast asleep. He slid off the bed and padded quietly over to the intensive-care ward. It was empty.

Worry shot through him like a red-hot knife through butter. Where was Lou? Where had they put her? He heard voices and hid behind the door as they came closer. "We'll transfer Lou back from recovery in the morning. If there's any change, bleep me immediately. I'm staying in my quarters on base tonight." The voices passed and Jim stood up. Where was recovery? He couldn't exactly ask and if he wandered around too much, he'd get caught.

A medic came out of a room at the far end and as the door closed, Jim got a glimpse of a bed and equipment. He waited until the coast was clear and then quickly moved across to it. He pushed the door open and went into a dimly lit room containing six beds and equipment. At the far corner, only one was occupied. A medic sat at the end of the bed.

Jim quietly sneaked down the ward, not really knowing what he'd do when he got there. He was almost there when the Tannoy sprang to life, making him jump. "Airman Willis, report to the main infirmary."

Jim dropped to the floor and hid just in time as the medic on duty got up and left the room. Jim darted across to Lou's bed. He looked sadly at the motionless figure and what was left of her leg. Then he sat next to the bed.

The monitors beeped quietly as he took hold of Lou's hand. "Hiya. You look like death warmed up, but I guess you only look as good as you feel. I'm sorry. If I hadn't been angry, none of this would have happened and you'd be OK and with the rest of us, not stuck in here on your own."

Now he was here, he didn't know what to say. "We've got an 'escort,' as General Merrick puts it. His name is Sergeant Peterson and he and Jack are best mates, it seems. I wouldn't be able to lose him in a blizzard. I can't stay long, because he's probably on my tail as I speak. Need to get back before Staci wakes and misses me anyway. Mum and Dad have grounded me for the rest of my life. At this rate I shall be ninety before anyone trusts me again."

The overhead lights flicked on, making him jump.

"Ninety-five," Jack told him furiously. "You'll be ninety-five before anyone trusts you again. You were told Lou was off limits tonight. Rules are made for a reason, not to be ignored or broken if you don't like them. And you are the *last* person I would have expected to pull a stunt like this. You keep insisting you're an adult, so act like one."

Jim's heart pounded and his stomach felt like a box of rocks as it sank into his shoes. "Sorry."

Dr. Andrews fixed him with an angry glare. "You are so fortunate your father isn't here right now. I'm within an inch of calling him. Perhaps I should do."

Jim shifted uncomfortably, his face burning. He

knew he was going to get yelled at, but even so hadn't expected it to be done in front of an audience. "How did you know where I was?"

"It wasn't rocket science!" Jack said. "We have security cameras everywhere on base, which made it easy to find you. The escort is for your protection as well as ours. Dr. Andrews had very good reasons for not wanting Lou to have visitors tonight."

Jim's face burned like it was on fire. "Sorry. I just wanted to see her and tell her what we did today. We've been together every minute of every day for so long now; it doesn't seem right without her."

"Go back to bed," Jack told him firmly. "Airman Thomas will take you."

Jim squeezed Lou's hand. "I'll see you tomorrow. By the way, you missed out on fast food. And there were so many cars in town. Ailsa had forgotten about traffic. The green man is white here. Weird."

"Jim. Bed, now," Jack said firmly. "Don't make me repeat myself, or we really will call your parents."

"I can always sedate you," Dr. Andrews added.

"OK. I'm going." He squeezed Lou's hand. "Good night, sleep tight, and don't let the bed bugs bi—" He broke off as Lou's fingers gently tightened on his hand. "Jack, she squeezed my hand."

Dr. Andrews went to the bed and shone a light in Lou's eyes. "Lou?" she said. "Can you hear me?"

"Go." Jack pointed at the door, his tone leaving no more room to maneuver.

Jim left the room, but waited in the hallway. He kept watch from the doorway.

Lou tried to move her head away from the light. Her fingers moved again and she moaned softly, coughing against the ventilator.

Dr. Andrews put the torch down and began to remove the ventilator.

Lou moved her head and moaned.

Dr. Andrews said, "Lou, can you hear me? Open your eyes for me."

Lou's eyes flickered open.

"Good girl." Dr. Andrews took her hands. "Can you squeeze my fingers for me?"

Lou did so.

"Well done." Dr. Andrews glanced across at a nurse. "Go get Mrs. Benson."

"She's in my quarters," Jack said. "I'll stay here with Lou. She'll need a familiar face."

The medic nodded and ran from the room.

Lou whispered, "It hurts."

"I can do something about that." Dr. Andrews injected something into the cannula. "Give it a few minutes and it should help."

Jack took her hand. "Hi," he said.

"Jack? Where am I?" Her voice, no louder than a whisper, was croaky.

"Anderson Air Force Base on Guam."

"I thought I dreamt you on the beach."

Jack smiled. "No. I'm quite real."

"Where's Mum?"

"She'll be here in a minute." He took the cup and straw from the medic. "Do you want a drink?"

"Please. My throat hurts."

"Just a sip." He lifted her head and held the cup as she took a mouthful. He laid her gently back on the pillows and put the cup down. Dr. Andrews injected something else into the drip and adjusted it.

"The others?"

"They're here, along with Bill and Di Kirk. Asleep,

or they should be. Jim—" Jack beckoned him over. "You can have two minutes, then go to bed."

Jim moved to Lou's side. "Hey…"

"Jim…"

"Yeah. I'm here."

"Not your fault," she whispered.

"Yes, it is."

"I don't blame you."

"Lou!" Footsteps ran down the ward.

Lou turned her head slightly. "Mum."

Jim stood back against the wall to keep out of the way. Tears burned his eyes. *Thank You, God.*

Nichola gathered her daughter in her arms. "Lou, I thought I'd lost you forever."

"I'm sorry, Mum."

Nichola finally released Lou from the hug and laid her back down on the pillows. "I am so mad at you," she said. "It was a stupid, thoughtless, selfish, cruel thing to do. Have you any idea what you put us through?"

"I didn't want Jim to go alone." Lou's face contorted with pain. "It hurts," she said. "My leg…"

"They couldn't save your leg, love," Nichola said gently.

"I never expected it to be fixable."

Dr. Andrews came over. "I'll give you something to make you sleep. That should help."

Lou tightened her grip on her mother's hand. "Don't go."

Nichola gripped her hand tightly. "I'm not going anywhere."

Jack tapped Jim on the shoulder. "You need to get some sleep as well, Jim. You can come and see her again in the morning. Stray again and the doc will carry out her threat."

Jim nodded. He was tired enough to sleep without sedation. "OK."

8

Lou slept fitfully, despite the sedative. She woke suddenly and looked at the clock. Half past six. She wondered if it were morning or evening, but figured morning as it was dark outside. The lights were dimmed and she was in a private room now rather than a huge ward. Her mother was gone. Perhaps the nurses had chased her to bed.

She lifted her head slightly and looked down at her legs.

She recoiled in shock and a sense of loss enveloped her, crushing her with a weight so heavy, she gasped involuntarily. It was gone. She could feel it, but it was gone.

A stab of grief plunged deep within her. What would she do now? She'd never walk again. She watched as her dreams vanished into the cloud that was descending over the bed. She could never become a world-famous archaeologist and find Atlantis or El Dorado now.

God must really hate her.

She looked out of the window. The sky was beginning to lighten and beyond the glass, the birds started to sing. Tears ran down her cheeks.

The medic on duty came over to her. "Are you OK?"

Lou shook her head.

"Shall I get your mom?"

Lou shook her head again. "No," she cried.

"Are you in pain?"

"A lot." She watched as the medic picked up the chart and took it to the desk.

Lou watched as the sky grew paler. Another dawn she didn't want to see. The medic came back. "I can't give you anything for another three hours."

"Sounds about right," she whispered. "Mafuso and Ailsa kept saying that too. All the time."

"I'll speak to Dr. Andrews when she comes on duty at 0700." The medic went back to the desk.

Lou wiped her eyes against the onslaught of tears, but it was a losing battle.

Despite the growing light outside, around Lou it seemed to grow darker. When breakfast came at 0700, she pushed it around the plate, but didn't eat anything.

Dr. Andrews came over. "Good morning. How are you?"

"Not hungry."

"Can I get you something else instead? Maybe some toast or some cereal?"

"No."

"The nurse tells me you need some pain meds?"

"Yeah," Lou said.

"I'll increase the dose slightly, but if you don't eat, you won't get better. Are you sure you don't want this? The others have done nothing but eat since they've been here."

"Just make sure they have enough. We're almost out of food again."

"We won't run out. There's plenty for you as well."

"I'm not hungry."

"I've got one of our trained counselors coming in

to see you—"

"I don't need a shrink because I'm not hungry," Lou snapped, interrupting her. "There is nothing to talk about. My life as it was is over. End of story." She turned away and shut her eyes.

As the footsteps moved away, she opened her eyes and lay with a fixed stare at the ceiling. She slowly moved her gaze across the tiles, counting the lights. Lots of them.

Dr. Andrews returned with the morphine. "It's not a full dose because it's too early still." She injected it and looked at Lou. "We'll get you mobile tomorrow."

Lou snorted. "Mobile? I can't walk, can I?"

"Wheelchair. We'll also organize some crutches and see about getting a prosthesis fitted."

"A what?"

"Artificial leg, but one thing at a time. Would you like to sit up a little?"

"OK."

Dr. Andrews picked up a control next to the bed and pressed one of the buttons. Slowly, the bed rose until she was sitting slightly.

"Thanks," Lou said.

"How's the leg doing?" Dr. Andrews asked.

"It hurts."

"Other than it hurts?"

Lou turned her head and looked at the doctor. "You mean aside from the fact that my leg isn't there?" *What's with the obvious questions?* She sucked in a deep breath. "Like I said, it hurts. And my toes itch."

Dr. Andrews examined the stump. "It's looking all right. We'll leave it uncovered today."

Lou grimaced. "Can't you at least hide it so I can't see it?"

"Sure we can. Be right back."

Lou sighed. Why was everyone being so nice to her when she didn't deserve it? It'd be best just to push everyone away so they wouldn't care so much when she died.

Because that was still going to happen. She knew that. Mafuso said so and no one had told her otherwise.

Dr. Andrews returned with a leg shield. She placed it over Lou's legs and arranged the covers so the stump was hidden from view but left uncovered. "How's that?"

"Better, thank you."

Dr. Andrews smiled. "Your mom will be in soon. I expect the others will be too. Can I get you something to read?"

"No thanks. I'll just sit here and look out the window."

About an hour later, footsteps echoed across the room. She turned as they came over. "Hi, guys," she said as Jim, Staci, and Ailsa came over.

"You look better," Jim said. "How're you doing?"

"Still here," Lou replied. "So what's happening then?" She nodded at the figures by the door. "Who are they?"

"The bloke is Sergeant Peterson and the woman is Staff Sergeant Chaney. They're our escorts," Ailsa explained.

Staci rolled her eyes. "They only gave us a woman so Sergeant Peterson doesn't have to go where no man has ever gone before...the ladies' room."

Ailsa and Staci sat on the bed and Jim sat in the chair next to it. Lou looked at them. "You have 'escorts'? Why?"

Jim grimaced. "General Merrick says they are for our 'protection' on the base, unquote. Really I think it's so we don't do a runner again."

"Who's General Merrick?"

"She's in charge of the base."

"So you guys can't go anywhere without an escort?"

"No, but then Mum and Dad are here as well."

Lou shifted on the bed. "Are they really here? Are they all right?"

Jim smiled. "They're fine. There was just no way for them to send a message home after the tsunami and quake. Once they did, we'd already left."

Staci nodded. "And they grounded us for like forever."

Lou looked thoughtful. "Mum was here. And Jack. He called her Nicky. No one ever does that, 'cept your parents."

"She's been staying at his place since she came out in December, along with Mum and Dad. They're obviously friends. Friends shorten each other's names," Jim said. "Like you call me Jim and I call you Lou. Rather than James and Louisa."

"Dad never did. He always called her Nichola."

"But then she always called him Robert and never Bob."

"True." She paused. "So what have you guys been up to?"

Jim pulled the big parcel out from the side of the bed and gave it to Lou. "We did this."

Lou opened it. Her picture looked wonderful in its new frame. Far better than she'd ever imagined when she sewed it. "Wow. Thank you."

"The girls chose the frame and mount, so if you

don't like it, blame them."

"It's lovely." She passed it to Ailsa. "Can you wrap it again for me? Then I can give it to Mum. Ta."

"We did other stuff too," Staci told her. "We went clothes shopping and we went to get fast food yesterday. Today we're going on a tour of the island."

"Sounds fun. Today I get to sit up."

Ailsa smiled at her. "Would you rather still be on Agrihan? I know I wouldn't."

As tempting as it was to shoot back a sarcastic answer or say yes, Lou just shook her head. Probably best not to upset the others by saying she'd rather not be here.

"It's strange having to do what grown-ups want again," Staci said. "Having done what I wanted for so long."

"Not even grown-ups can do what they want *all* the time," Jim told her. "All the grown-ups here have to do what General Merrick tells them. She's only asking of us what she expects from everyone here."

"What's going to happen when you leave here?" Lou asked.

Jim shrugged. "For the time being, our parents are all staying at Jack's place in town along with Nichola, but long term, Mum and Dad inherited Aunt Edith's house, so that's us sorted. I don't know where you'll go. Nichola sold the flat."

Lou looked at him, aghast. "She sold it? Why?"

"You'll have to ask her that when she comes in later. But like I said, once we're released from the infirmary, we'll be moving into Jack's place until Mum and Dad go back to England."

Sergeant Peterson came over to them. "We'd better be going."

They said their goodbyes and followed Sergeant Peterson from the room, Staff Sergeant Chaney falling in behind.

Lou looked at the clock. Another ten minutes and she could have some more morphine. She wondered briefly if they'd give her too much or if she could persuade them to, but she reckoned pigs stood a better chance of flying than she had of doing that. She had an improved view out of the window now she was sitting up. A plane came in and landed and another one took off.

The medic came over. She chatted as she checked the dosage on the morphine pump and changed one of the bags that constantly dripped into her arm. She had no idea what it was, most likely antibiotics or something. Had Mum told them what she was allergic to? Otherwise, they'd be in for a shock.

The sun blazed down outside and if she listened carefully, she could still hear the birds over the sounds of the infirmary and the planes. She thanked the nurse before she left and then turned her thoughts to what Jim had said about Mum selling the flat. Why would she do that? How could she do that? It was her home, too. Mum had no right to sell it without consulting her.

Lou brooded on this and when Mum came to visit her just after 11 AM, her anger spilled over the moment she saw her mother entering the ward. "Why did you do it? How could you sell the flat like that? Where are we meant to live now?"

9

"Good morning to you, too, Lou." The smile on Mum's face froze and then fell as the full force of Lou's anger hurtled across the ward at her.

"It was my home!" Lou huffed. "How could you sell it without telling me?"

Mum narrowed her eyes. "Let me at least sit down first."

Lou waited until her mother had sat next to the bed, and then folded her arms tightly across her chest. Bile rose up her throat and she had to force it back down. Throwing up wouldn't help any. She needed answers, not sympathy. "Well?"

"You have no idea what I've been through, have you? We were going to sell it anyway."

"But you did it without telling me."

"You weren't there, Lou. You ran away. You walked out without a goodbye, on a half-baked rescue plan none of you had thought through properly. I had no idea what to do. I was stuck in a flat full of memories I couldn't cope with. I didn't know if you were alive or dead. I stayed there as long as I could. I sold it to have money to search for you."

Mum paused. "Jack rang me after he met you in Cornwall, but then you vanished again before he could get a message to you. He called again after he ran into you on Grand Turk. I asked him to pay for the boat repairs, and I wired him the money to do so. I wanted to go out there and bring you back, but trying to get a flight was hopeless. Jack and I had a long talk on the phone. That call lasted two hours. He said he'd keep an eye on you while he could, until I could get out there, but you left the day before my plane was due to leave. Jack said the best thing I could do was stay in England. After that he rang me once a week. I was a mess. Jack was a friend when I needed one the most."

Lou scowled. "Thought he was mine."

Mum continued. "Bill and Di got back to the UK in September and they were just as worried as I was. Never mind traumatized because of what they'd been through. They moved into Edith's place and I sold the flat. All the furniture went into storage and I moved in with them. Jack called in early December. He'd found the wreck of your boat while flying a routine recon mission. It had been swept clear of the rocks you'd hit and had wound up on the rocks of Pagan—the next island in the chain. They spent days searching it for you. The three of us flew out here a week before Christmas. Jack met us at the airport, and we've been staying at his place ever since. We wanted to be here when they found you."

Lou looked at the window. "Are you living there now?" she asked icily.

"Right now, I'm using his quarters here on the base, but yes, I am. We all are."

"You can't just replace Dad like that."

"It's not like that."

"You're living in his house, staying in his quarters. What *is* it like then?"

Mum glared at her. "Jack is a friend. Nothing more."

"Yeah, right," Lou said rudely. "I didn't think you

Christians did things like that. Living together is a sin, isn't it?"

"Don't you dare question me, Louisa. Bill and Di are staying there too. You ran away, or don't you remember that?"

Lou's eyes stung with tears. "You can't even be honest with me now, can you? I saw the way he looked at you last night. He fancies you. He shortens your name. And you looked at him the same way. You held his hand."

Dr. Andrews came over and took Lou's wrist to take her pulse and shoved a thermometer in her mouth. She smiled at Mum. "I just need to run a few checks. Can you give me a few minutes? I won't be long," she said.

"That's OK," Mum said. "I have to pop out for a sec anyway." She got up and left the room quickly.

Lou watched her go. "I haven't seen her for months and she's mad at me already," she muttered around the thermometer.

Dr. Andrews looked at Lou. "You need to ease up on your mom, young lady. She's been through a very difficult time these past months. Her friends were missing, presumed killed, and then you three go off on some fantasy adventure to find them. She thought you were dead."

Lou snorted derisively. "She sure got over it quick. Moved in with someone I thought was a friend."

"If you mean Colonel Fitzgerald, you're reading the situation wrong. He's a gentleman and a good friend. He would never do anything to hurt your mom. You need to listen to what she has to say, rather than yelling. That isn't going to do your blood pressure any good," Dr. Andrews said. She put the thermometer away and pulled back the covers to check Lou's leg.

"Aren't I too young to have to worry about that?"

"Keep the yelling up and you'll be back in surgery quicker than you can count to five," Dr. Andrews said firmly.

Mum came back in. Her face was blotchy, as if she'd been crying.

Dr. Andrews smiled and replaced the covers. "All done here. It's looking much better."

"That's good." Mum nodded as she sat down by Lou's bed again.

Dr. Andrews lingered for a moment longer as she wrote up the chart. "OK. You remember what I said, young lady." She headed back to her office.

Mum looked at Lou. "What did she say?"

"Told me to shut up before I burst a blood vessel," Lou paraphrased.

"She has a point," her mother said. She twisted her hands on her lap. "Concerning Jack. Yes, I like him. A lot. As you so crudely put it, I fancy him. But, sweetheart, neither of us are going to compromise our faith by living together in the way you were insinuating. I loved your father, Lou. We were married for seventeen years. That's almost half my lifetime and a year longer than yours. You don't just forget that or throw it away without a care or second thought. When he died three years ago, I didn't think I'd ever love again. You were my whole life." She paused. "Things change, sometimes when you least expect them. Jack has asked me to stay here with him, instead of going back to England."

Lou watched her mother carefully. "What about me?"

"Of course you will be there too. Jack's place is

huge. He wants both of us."

"Are we talking marriage here, or just living together?" Lou kept her voice level this time.

"Right now, we're dating. I sleep in the guest room. There is nothing untoward going on. I promise. Even if Bill and Di weren't in the same house, there wouldn't be."

Lou picked at the edge of the blanket. She could either prolong the argument and upset her mother further or she could make it look like she'd given in. "I like Jack. I'm not going to object to you seeing him. Just promise me no more secrets."

Mum hugged her. "I promise. No more secrets."

Jack came across from Dr. Andrews's office. "Good morning," he said.

"Morning, Uncle Jack," Lou said.

Jack raised an eyebrow. "*Uncle* Jack?"

"Isn't that the title you give to the man your mum is going out with?" Lou replied innocently.

He looked at Mum. "You told her then, Nicky?"

"Yeah."

Jack smiled. "Good. And there's no need to call me uncle. Just Jack will do fine."

Lou shrugged. "Weird name choice, but OK, Just Jack."

Jack rolled his eyes as he sat on Lou's bed. "Lou, there's something I want you to know. When I asked your mom to stay here with me, she agreed on two conditions. Nothing would happen between us, and she came as a package with you. I have no intentions of replacing your dad. Now or ever."

Lou blushed. "You heard that?"

"I think the entire base did." He took Mum's hand and looked at Lou. "I love your mother. I have from the moment I met her. I asked her to stay because I don't want her to go."

Lou put her hand on top of theirs. "It's OK, Jack. I don't mind. So long as you don't do anything untoward towards her, it's fine. Have you told Jim and Staci?"

"Bill and Di know, but we haven't exactly been hiding our relationship. I haven't said anything to the others yet. I wanted to tell you first," Mum said.

Dr. Andrews came over. "General Merrick would like to see Lou now, if possible. Then I need to run a few more tests."

Mum nodded and stood up. "I'll come back this afty."

Jack got up too and saluted as General Merrick came over.

General Merrick returned his salute. She waited until they had left the room before sitting next to Lou's bed. She then gave Lou the same lecture that Lou assumed she had given the others.

Lou sat silently through it, hearing but not listening. She was quite adept at that, having perfected it at school. She nodded in the right places and apologized for wasting so much of everyone's time.

"Answer me one thing," General Merrick said. "Back in June, when you ran away, there was an incident at the docks in Southampton. A police boat exploded, killing two officers. Three were saved by a girl from a passing cabin cruiser. She gave her name as Louisa Benson. The name of the boat was *Avon*, call sign Alpha-Juliet-Tango-Kilo. I assume it was you?"

Lou nodded. "Yeah. Jim didn't want to help and was furious because I did."

"You risked your life for total strangers. You also

put your whole journey in jeopardy."

"That's why Jim was so cross. Seems like a lifetime ago. But it isn't like I'll be doing that again any time soon."

"Why not?"

Lou pulled the covers aside and pointed to the remains of her leg. "That's why not. I made a mistake five months ago and I shall pay for it as long as I live." She stifled a yawn. She didn't want to be rude, but she was suddenly very tired.

"I'll let you get some sleep." General Merrick stood up. "Is there is anything I can do?"

"I could do with the morphine upped. It's not touching the pain."

"I'll let the doctor know on my way out. Is there anything else?"

"No, General." She paused. "I'm sorry; pain makes me cranky and not very good company."

"You're not alone on that score, as pain makes me cranky, too." General Merrick nodded and rose.

Lou resumed gazing out of the window. The planes were still taking off and landing frequently. She saw Jack and three others, including a petite blonde, cross the tarmac and climb into a helicopter. It sat with rotors turning and then took off. Lou took a deep breath, wishing she could scratch her toes. They really did itch something chronic.

"Lou?"

She turned her head. "Yes, Dr. Andrews?"

"Time for those tests," Dr. Andrews said.

"Great." Lou rolled her eyes.

"That's what Staci said, with more or less the same expression on her face, too. We ran the same tests on all the others. Sooner we start, the sooner we're done."

Dr. Andrews put a tray of instruments down and pulled the curtains around the bed. "This is the part Colonel Fitzgerald always refers to as the human pincushion bit. If it's any consolation, he hates it, as well."

"OK." Lou held out her arm, not seeing the point in objecting.

Clare Revell

10

It was evening when they wheeled her back to the infirmary from yet another scan.

Mum sat by the bed, waiting for her. "Hi, sweetheart," she said. "You OK?"

"I guess so."

"I can get you some dinner if you want."

Lou shook her head. Just the thought of food made her stomach turn itself in knots. Part of her knew that was down to hunger, but the other part of her wasn't going to risk eating just in case. "No thanks. I'm more tired than hungry."

"You need to eat."

Lou tilted her head. "I'll be sick if I do, which is kind of a waste of food. I have something for you." She pointed. "That package next to the unit there."

Mum picked it up. "This one?"

Lou nodded. Perhaps this would get Mum off the food kick. She watched as Mum opened it. "I made it on the boat on the journey here."

Mum's eyes glistened as she gazed at the cross-stitch picture of the white horses on the beach. "Oh, sweetheart…"

"I wanted you to have it."

"Thank you." Mum put the picture on the table and hugged her. "I love it. I shall hang it in my room."

Lou hugged her back and leaned against the pillows as Mum released her from the hug. "Is Jack

68

back yet?"

"No, how did you know he was gone?"

"Window faces the runway. When's he due back?"

"Tomorrow morning. Why?"

Lou shrugged. "No reason. Just wondered."

Mum studied her for a moment. Whatever she was working up to saying wasn't going to be good. "Dr. Andrews wants you to talk to one of the counselors they have here."

"I already told her no."

"Lou, she's worried about you. So am I. I've read the logbook you and Jim kept."

"That's more than I have." Lou looked down at the covers. That meant everyone would have read it. Including her backwards entries, because there wasn't going to be a shortage of mirrors here.

Mum sighed. "You're like a different person now. You willingly risked your life in June for three people you didn't know. Your log entries read fluently. You sound happy, full of life and love and vitality. Then after the shark it all changes."

"That's because everything *did* change. Life did a huge U-turn. Nothing was the same after that."

Mum frowned, as if she wasn't sure how to broach the subject. "Lou, love, it sounds like you were really sick. Did you really want to stay behind?"

"Yes. If you read the logs, then you know I'm dying. The others didn't need to see that. And you wouldn't want me back just to lose me again. It was better for everyone if I stayed behind with Deefer."

"That's why you need to talk to someone. Just like all the others have done already. You've been through a lot."

"I don't need a shrink. How many times do I have

to say it?"

"I'm not saying you do, but you need —"

"What I need are painkillers that actually work. I'm tired of the pain. And I wish my leg would stop itching for just five seconds. I just want it to go away. I want everything to go away. I wanna be left alone."

Mum smiled faintly. "That's my girl, always cranky when she's hurting. OK, love. I'll come back and see you tomorrow." She got up and kissed Lou's forehead. "Night, love."

"Night, Mum."

Mum picked up the picture. She paused at the doorway. "Lou, love, you're not dying." She headed out of the room.

"Yes, I am," Lou whispered. "Mafuso said so and no doctor has said otherwise." She turned her head to face the wall and closed her eyes. If only her foot would stop itching for a few minutes, it'd help.

11

Jim and Ailsa ate dinner together with Nichola and his parents in the mess. Staci was already asleep in the main infirmary. Jim hoped they could move into Jack's place the following day. It wasn't that he didn't like being here; he just wanted to be alone with his parents and away from the constant supervision of armed guards. Even though he hadn't done anything wrong, other than sneaking out to see Lou when he'd been told not to, their presence made him feel guilty anyway.

As they finished eating, Nichola looked over at Jim. "Could you do me a favor? Go and see Lou and see if you can talk some sense into her? I can't seem to say anything right at the moment."

"I'll try," he said.

"Thank you. And tell her you've all spoken to the counselor already. She thinks we're picking on her. Oh, she hasn't said as much, but I know the way she thinks."

"I'll try. See you in a bit." He stood and headed down to the infirmary, with Sergeant Peterson following.

Lou lay with her eyes closed.

Jim sat next to her bed. "Hi," he said. "I know you're awake."

"I'm asleep," came the reply. She gave a couple of mock snores. "See, sleeping."

"When are you going to stop this spoilt-brat act of yours?"

Lou opened her eyes and looked at him. "My *what*?" she asked.

He noticed the hollow, dead look was back. His stomach churned and he swallowed hard. He thought they'd gotten past this. "It's time you grew up and stopped acting like a child. We've put your mum through enough without you carrying on like this."

Lou pushed up on her elbows and glared at him. "How *dare* you talk to me like that?"

"Well, no one else will. I put up with it on the boat and on Agrihan because I had no choice. Plus which, I had Staci to consider. And I cut you some slack after Deefer died, but no more. You want to cut yourself off and sulk like a baby because you can't have your own way, then feel free. Don't come crying to me, because you won't get any sympathy."

Lou shook her head at him. "I have every right to feel like this. I'm dying."

"Codswallop," Jim snapped. "The doctors here worked jolly hard to stop the infection and succeeded, I may add. The antibiotics you're on are finishing the job."

Lou scowled. "Fine then. I will never walk again. Oh, they are talking wheelchairs and wooden legs and crutches, but it's not the same. You don't know what it's like, so don't you dare start on me. It's like a nightmare, but you can't tell where the dream stops and reality starts."

"Which is why you need to talk to someone."

"Oh, for Pete's sake. Don't you start on that as well."

Jim rolled his eyes. "Actually, they made us all go

talk to the counselor. It wasn't as bad as it sounds. She just sat there and listened."

"I'm not doing it. I put all my thoughts in the logbook; don't need to rehash the whole experience again. Just leave me alone." She turned away and shut her eyes.

Jim got up. "With pleasure." He left the infirmary and went back to the others. He sat down and shook his head. "I don't know I did any good. Probably not."

"Thanks for trying." Nichola sighed. "The only person who might get through is Jack. He said she opened up a bit on the island. I'll get him to go see her tomorrow once he gets back."

****

In the infirmary Lou lay looking up at the ceiling. Was Jim right about her not dying now? Mum had said the same thing. She didn't understand why the doctor or any of the nurses hadn't said anything if it were true.

Perhaps Jim was just saying it because he wanted her to stop feeling sorry for herself.

As a medic passed, Lou asked for an envelope and some notepaper. The medic gave her some along with a pen. Lou chewed on the pen lid for a moment, then began to write. It took several attempts until she was sure it was right. She shoved it in the envelope and wrote *Colonel Jack Fitzgerald* on the front. She put it on the bedside table, then destroyed the other attempts. She put the notebook on top of the letter and closed her eyes.

She heard someone come in, but pretended she was asleep. She didn't want another lecture. There had been way too many of them for one day.

****

The following morning, Lou once again refused breakfast. Just the smell of the food on the tray the doctor held turned her stomach. "I'm not hungry."

Dr. Andrews rolled her eyes. "Then you need to drink something. Otherwise, you can't have more painkillers."

Lou huffed. "Fine. Tea, white with two sugars."

The doctor just stood there. "And what's the magic word?"

Lou shook her head. "You sound just like my mother. Please."

Dr. Andrews smiled. "Sure. And my mother did the same thing to me. It must be a universal parental tactic to make us say please." She disappeared, taking the tray with her. She soon returned with a cup. "Here you go."

"Thank you." Lou wrapped her hands around the cup, relishing the warmth.

"On a scale of one to ten, one being no pain and ten being pretty bad, how's your leg this morning?"

"Not there," she replied flatly.

Dr. Andrews raised an eyebrow. "Really?"

Lou sipped the tea. "Yeah, really. Even I can see that my leg is no longer there and I'm just a kid, not a doctor."

The doctor smiled. "OK, let me rephrase the question. How is your pain level?"

"Nine." She swallowed. "Can I ask you something?"

The doctor perched on the edge of the bed. "Sure,

if I can ask something in return."

"OK." She figured she'd probably regret agreeing to that, but oh well. "Am I still dying?"

"Dying? What makes you think that?"

"I heard you talking several times when I was sleeping. About me not making it. And besides, Mafuso said the same thing. That my leg was too bad and the infection would kill me."

Dr. Andrews nodded. "It would have done if you hadn't been rescued when you were, and yes, you were pretty sick. You crashed about three or four times, and it was touch and go for a few hours when you first got here, but you're doing fine now."

"Really?" she whispered.

"Yeah, really. There's no sign of infection and the meds I'm giving you will get rid of what bugs are left in your system. There's no reason why you won't live to be ninety or so."

Lou looked at her. She wasn't sure if she were relieved or not. "OK. You wanted to ask something in return."

Dr. Andrews pulled out her notebook. "What did you use for pain meds on the island?"

"Ailsa made something with a plant. She called it mytona. It was brilliant stuff. At least to start with, 'cause it numbed the pain for hours. It tasted disgusting though. You'll have to ask her what plant it was. Mafuso did the same."

"You mentioned him just now. He was the medic in the village?"

Lou took a deep drink of the tea. The only problem now her stomach had something in it, it wanted more. But it couldn't have it. Her stubborn streak kicked in hard. She'd said no to breakfast, so that was the end of it. "Yeah, he was." She set the cup down. "One of the good guys."

"You liked him?"

"He's married, so it's irrelevant."

"I didn't mean like him, like him." Dr. Andrews grinned. "But it makes it easier to respond to people when you get along with them."

Lou nodded slightly.

"I had this boss once...not on this base, but another one. He was an ogre."

"Really?" An image of a green monster in uniform floated through Lou's mind.

"Oh, yeah. Annoy him and he'd have you cleaning things with a toothbrush."

"I didn't think they could do that." Lou glanced up. "What kind of things?"

"Floors, sinks, even toilets."

Lou scrunched up her nose. "Yuck."

Dr. Andrews nodded. "Definitely. I haven't had to make any of my staff do that yet. A couple of patients got threatened with it, mind you." She lowered her voice. "Colonel Fitzgerald for one."

"Really?" Lou tried not to appear too interested, but she was. And part of her was enjoying the conversation now they weren't talking about her.

"He won't turn up for medicals. He'll do all he can to avoid post-mission checks. And as for shots? You can forget it. I'm thinking he's afraid of needles, but won't admit it. Just don't tell him I told you that. You finished with the tea?"

Lou nodded.

"Want some more?"

She shook her head.

"OK." Dr. Andrews picked up the cup and took it

away. She returned with a wheelchair. "Care to go for a ride?"

"Do I have a choice?"

"No. This time, we'll lift you out of the bed, but tomorrow you'll learn how to get into and out of the chair yourself. That way, you'll get some independence back." Dr. Andrews put the brakes on the chair and pulled back the covers. She disconnected the morphine pump.

Lou didn't even get time to open her mouth to object before the medic lifted her and put her in the chair. She bit her lip as pain soared through her thigh and she averted her gaze from the stump where her lower leg used to be.

Dr. Andrews put a blanket round Lou's legs. "Airman Ryder will take you out. He'll also show you how to wheel yourself." She attached the drip to the chair. "See you later."

Airman Ryder pushed Lou out of the infirmary. "Where to?" he asked.

"You're driving," Lou told him.

"You're navigating."

"I don't know where anything is. I haven't left the infirmary since I got here." She paused, pointing to the door. "How about we go that way?"

Airman Ryder chuckled. "That's a great help. There must be something on the base you want to see."

Lou waited a moment, not wanting it to be too obvious she was keen to get outside. "Then go out of the door and turn left. Can we go and find the runway? We could watch the planes come in and take off."

"I can't do that, because it's a restricted area, but we'll find somewhere nice to sit in the sunshine."

Airman Ryder pushed her down the corridor and

to the lift. They went to the ground floor and outside where the sun shone brightly and the breeze ruffled Lou's hair.

Lou sucked in a deep breath, trying not to show how good it was to be in the fresh air and out of the horrid clinical, antiseptic environment of the infirmary.

Airman Ryder pushed her slowly across to the base shops, explaining how to push herself. He parked the chair under a tree overlooking the car park.

Lou sighed. This guy had a strange definition of "somewhere nice" but she wasn't going to argue with him. Jack waved at her from across the car park. She nodded to him, trying not to smile as he jogged over to her.

"Hi, Lou. How are you doing?"

Lou shrugged. "I'm here. How are you?"

"I'm here as well," Jack replied. "So that makes three of us. Couldn't you find a nicer view though?"

Lou rolled her eyes. "I'm not driving," she deadpanned. "I'm just going where I'm pushed. Airman Ryder chose the parking space."

Airman Ryder said, "Doc Andrews wanted to see you when you got back, sir."

Lou looked at him. "Must be nice to be wanted."

"That's why they call me Mr. Popularity." Jack smiled. "Would you like to get some lunch later, Lou?"

"I'll see if I can fit you into my busy schedule." She tilted her head. "You know, between tests and more tests and watching cars drive across the tarmac and park between white lines."

Jack shook his head. "Better go and see the doc. Don't have too much fun out here."

"No chance of that," Lou told him. "Have fun with Dr. Andrews. Mind she doesn't give you a toothbrush."

He gave her a funny look, but she didn't bother explaining.

Instead, she reached down to scratch her leg and then sighed as her hand met nothing but air. That was going to take some getting used to.

12

Lou watched Jack's retreating figure as he headed back across the grass to the main building.

"Do you want something to drink?" Airman Ryder asked.

Lou shook her head. "No, I'm fine. I had some tea just before we came out. Maybe later though."

"Nice view of the car park," Staci said.

Lou hadn't even heard her walk up. Ailsa arrived next, with Jim hanging back.

"Seen one car, you seen them all," Lou answered. "And no one can park in one attempt either."

They sat in silence. Then Ailsa tried. "We're off to the beach. The Kirks are meeting us here. Jim's going to teach me how to play volleyball. Do you want to come?"

"I've never been any good at volleyball. 'Sides, they wouldn't let me today. Sand and raw wounds aren't a good combination. Nor are wheelchairs and sand, come to think of it."

Jim nodded. "Maybe next time then."

"Yeah, maybe." Lou sucked in a deep breath. "Though I thought you'd have had enough of beaches and sand by now."

Staci shook her head. "I can never have enough of beaches," she said. "Volcanoes and escorts, on the other hand..." She winked at Sergeant Peterson.

He chuckled. "Cheeky beggar, aren't you?"

Lou raised an eyebrow. That didn't sound very American to her.

"Staci's determined to teach me what she terms 'proper English,'" he said dryly.

Jim looked up and waved at one of the parked cars. "Mum and Dad are here. C'mon, let's go. You sure you don't want to come, Lou?"

She nodded. "I'm sure. Thanks for asking though."

He stood up, pulled Staci to her feet, and grabbed Ailsa's hand. "Better not keep Mum and Dad waiting. We'll see you when we get back. Have fun." They moved away, Sergeant Peterson and Staff Sergeant Chaney moving in to escort them.

Staci looked back. "Bye, Lou," she called.

Lou raised a hand in a halfhearted wave. "Bye." She watched them go and sighed. Why did things have to get so complicated all of a sudden? And why did everyone keep on telling her to have fun when she'd been parked in the most boring place on the base? No, make that the most boring place on the face of the planet.

She let her hand fall over the edge of the chair and ran her fingers over the brake lever. How difficult would it be to push the chair herself? It hadn't sounded too complicated when Airman Ryder explained it, but then neither had simultaneous quadratic equations in her maths class. And they were impossible.

She lifted her face to the sunshine and watched as a plane flew in low over the base, heading to the runway. She wasn't dying. The thought resounded round her mind.

She wasn't dying.

But was the chair an improvement? Could she ever come to terms with how fast things had changed?

Perhaps given time, she could. And let's face it, time was now something she had plenty of.

The wind ruffled her hair and she pushed a hand through it, wishing she had a hairband to tie it back with.

Another airman came across and sat next to Airman Ryder. They struck up an animated conversation, both men sitting with their backs to her.

Maybe she should try pushing this chair on her own. How had Dr. Andrews termed it? Getting her independence back, wasn't it? She pulled the brake lever back and, putting her hands on the wheels, pushed them. The chair moved slightly. *Hmmm, easier than it looks.*

She pushed against the wheels and moved the chair away from the trees, across the grass. *Not going far, just want to get the hang of this. Show off to Dr. Andrews when I get back inside. She'll be stoked.* She went a little farther, then looked over her shoulder at the way she had come.

Airman Ryder was still busy talking and hadn't noticed she'd gone.

Question was, how was she going to get back up the slope to him? She had no idea how to turn the chair around and her pride wouldn't allow her to call him for help. Besides, he'd probably think she was running away again or something stupid like that and just yell at her.

Maybe she should head over to the parking area. Once on the tarmac, it might be easier to do a three-point turn and hopefully she'd be back before he'd noticed she'd gone.

Her hand caught in the wheel and Lou yanked hard. Pain shot through her fingers as her hand finally came free. She rubbed it and realized it felt different. Glancing down, she discovered blood trickling down from the needle mark in the back of her hand. "Idiot," she told herself. "You pulled the drip out. The doc ain't gonna be stoked now."

She glanced over the side of the chair. The IV lay on the ground. "How'd you manage that?" Shaking her head, she reached down and put the brake on. Then she leaned over the side of the chair in an effort to pick up the IV bag.

The ground was a lot farther away than it looked. Lou leaned farther and the chair tipped, sending her toppling to the ground. She cried out in pain as she hit the ground with a thud. The chair landed beside her and she lay there, unable to do anything.

Tears of frustration and pain filled her eyes.

"Lou!" Jack's voice came from somewhere behind her.

Great. Just what I need. He's bound to take this the wrong way and yell at me now.

Pounding feet reached her and shiny black shoes appeared in her field of vision. "Are you hurt?"

"No. Just having a rest," she snapped, rubbing a hand over her eyes. "I thought I'd see the car park from a different angle."

"Very funny. Don't move till Doc Andrews gets here."

Lou looked up at him. "Why?" she asked, wondering why his dark eyes glinted in a mixture of anger and concern.

"Do you really need to ask? You could have undone all her hard work," Jack replied angrily. Footsteps came running from all directions. Jack held up his hand. "It's OK. I've got her." Someone stood up

Lou tried to roll over and sit up. "Put me back in the chair," she whispered, blinking back the tears. "Not lying here listening to this…"

Jack pushed her back down. "Don't you dare move."

Dr. Andrews came running across with her med bag.

Jack said, "Let the doc make sure you're OK. Then you and I are having a conversation. Over lunch."

Lou looked away. She wasn't going to be lectured for something she didn't do. She wasn't running away. She'd been there, done that, and had the scars to prove it.

Jack squatted down in front of her. "We are having…" he began.

Lou looked away again, wincing as Dr. Andrews re-sited the drip.

Jack took her face in his hands and forced her to look at him. "We are having this conversation whether you like it or not. Airman Ryder was good enough to bring you out and this is how you repay him. Don't you ever think of anyone but yourself? You owe him an apology."

Lou rolled her eyes. "I didn't do anything." However, she looked at Airman Ryder. "Sorry."

He nodded.

Jack looked at him. "Go get some coffee and leave the report on my desk. I'll deal with it."

"Yes, sir." He headed off.

"Is he in trouble?" Lou asked, wondering why a report was necessary.

"Yes. He was meant to be watching you and you could have gotten yourself killed because he was busy

84

talking."

"It's hardly a busy car park. I wasn't in any danger of getting killed. Besides, it wasn't his fault," Lou tried to explain.

"I don't want to hear it." Jack frowned. "Have you eaten?"

Lou looked away. It didn't seem to matter what she said, it was wrong. So it'd be best not to say anything.

Jack looked at Dr. Andrews. "Doc?"

"She hasn't eaten since she's been here." Dr. Andrews refastened the bandage around Lou's leg. "I'm done. You got off lightly, young lady. You haven't done any damage at all." She straightened up.

Jack picked Lou up and set her in the chair. He tucked the blanket around her legs, then turned to Dr. Andrews. "Do you want her back in bed or can I have a few words with her first?"

"That's fine, Colonel. You can have all the words you want with her. Bring her back at 1530."

"Aye, ma'am." Jack started to push Lou towards the main building. "First, we are having lunch."

"I'm not hungry."

"Fine. I'm having lunch. You can watch. Then after lunch we have to talk."

****

In the mess hall Jack pushed Lou's chair up to one of the tables. "What do you want?" he asked.

"I told you," Lou said slowly. "I'm not hungry."

Jack put the brake on. "Stay," he ordered and headed to the counter.

"I'm not a dog," Lou muttered. Why did these

people keep bothering? She wasn't worth it. She knew that. Even God knew that, because He'd let her get hurt this badly in the first place.

"Back." Jack put a tray with two plates of breaded chicken strips, French fries, and two cans of soda on the table. He put one plate in front of Lou and the other opposite her. "For once the line wasn't too long."

He put one of the forks by her plate. He sat opposite Lou and opened his can. He took a long drink and then picked up his fork. He ignored her as he began to eat. "It's good," he told her as he swallowed the first mouthful of food. "Try some."

Lou looked round the room at everyone else. They were talking and laughing, eating and drinking, having a good time with their friends and colleagues. She felt so alone, despite Jack sitting across from her. There was nothing like a crowd for making loneliness glaringly obvious.

The smell of the chicken made her mouth water. Her stomach rumbled. She glanced at Jack. He was halfway through his lunch. She looked down at the plate in front of her. It was easier to refuse food when she was on her own. She was starving, but it meant there wouldn't be enough for everyone else.

"How long is it since you've eaten?"

"Not since Deefer died. January 17," Lou muttered. "There wasn't much food and that way, it lasted the others longer. I don't know what today is."

"January 24," Jack told her. "Seven days."

"Is that all? Seems like a lifetime."

Jack picked up her fork. He stabbed the chicken and raised it to her mouth. "Open," he said. "I will feed you if I have to do so."

Lou opened her mouth and Jack shoved the

forkful of food inside it. Lou closed her mouth and Jack removed the fork.

He held her gaze. "Now eat it."

Lou took in his determined look and obediently chewed and swallowed, managing to gag as she did so.

"Eat or I *will* feed you."

Lou took the fork from his hand. "I'll do it myself."

Jack watched as she took the first mouthful. "No one is going to run out of food here," he said, softening his tone. "I promise, there is more than enough to go around. You can have seconds if you want."

She somehow finished what was in her mouth without gagging and looked at the plate. This amount of food would have had to have fed two of them, even though it was obviously a small portion. She blinked hard and stabbed at one of the fries.

He finished eating his own, watching her eat. Then he picked up his can and drank his cola thoughtfully.

Lou ate mechanically and very slowly. After five mouthfuls, she put down the fork down. "I've had enough," she said.

"Eat it," Jack commanded.

Lou scowled at him. "I'm not one of your airmen. You can't order me to do anything. And I'm not a baby, before you suggest feeding me again."

"Then stop acting like one and eat your lunch. Because me feeding you like a baby is a whole lot better than the alternative the doc is going to use unless you eat that food."

Lou sighed and picked up the fork. The meal was delicious and she was hungry. It was just the principle of it. Jack wasn't going to budge though, so she reluctantly began to eat.

Jack watched every mouthful. When she had finished, he handed her the soda. "Drink," he ordered.

She did as she was told, not wanting to refuse, in case he made good on his threat to feed her.

"Thank you. Now sit tight and don't move a muscle. I'll be right back." Jack put the empty plates away and pushed her down the corridor.

"Now what?" she asked.

"Now we talk."

"There's nothing to talk about."

Jack swung her round and backed through the double doors. "That's where you're wrong," he told her. "You don't want to talk to a counselor or your mom. Fine, but you're going to talk to me. If nothing else, you can explain that idiotic stunt you just pulled."

13

Lou closed her eyes as Jack swung the chair around again and headed out into the sunshine. The sun was warm on her face and the wind blew her hair everywhere, but she didn't care.

Talking wasn't going to help. The sooner he yelled at her and got it over with, the better it'd be. She sighed. And today had seemed so good at one point. Sitting in the sunshine and managing to do one thing for herself, then everything went downhill.

She rested a hand on her stomach, suddenly realizing that she no longer felt hungry and the gnawing pain in her tummy had gone.

Jack crossed the car park and headed into a building on the other side. He went through a few more fire doors and then stopped at a door at the end of the corridor. He took a key out of his pocket, unlocked the door, and pushed her inside.

"Where are we?" she asked.

"My quarters. We won't be disturbed here." Jack shut the door and pushed her across the room. He stopped the chair by the bed. He sat on the edge of the bed and looked at her. "Talk to me," he said.

Lou glanced around the room. Her mother's perfume and hairbrush sat on the dresser. Her robe was slung over the end of the bed and a small overnight bag rested on the chair. "Are you sure you're not living with my mother?"

"Quite sure." Jack looked at her. "Lou, we're both Christians and that kind of a relationship is designed for marriage only. At my place we have separate rooms."

"And here?"

"I'm crashing in the guest quarters for now. It's not ideal, but your mom needs to be near you and she wants me nearby too." He paused. "So, wanna tell me why you're so determined to leave now we've found you?"

"I wasn't leaving," she whispered.

Jack reached into his pocket and pulled out the crumpled letter. He waved it at her. "What's this then?" he demanded.

Her stomach twisted. *No...* "Where did you get that?"

"Dr. Andrews gave it to me—that's why she wanted to see me. She said it had been left there for me." He opened it and started reading. "*Jack. This is the fourth attempt to write this. I can't even do that properly and if I can't even write a simple letter, what chance do I have of doing anything right ever again? That's why it has to be this way. It is better for everyone if I go now, before things go anymore wrong or crazy than they already have. It's not fair on the others or on Mum for things to carry on the way they are right now. It has to be this way, don't you see? There is no other way. I can't do this anymore. I have reached the limit of what I can cope with. It's too dark, the arguments with myself too loud. I can't move or breathe. It's all encompassing, all embracing. There is no way out— except one. The decision has been made. Fear has gone. Emptiness remains. Joy defeated, life vanquished, sorrow victorious. No point in carrying on. Take care of Mum. Lou.*"

Lou sighed. She should have thrown the stupid note away. Things had changed since she'd written that. "You weren't supposed to get that. Why couldn't she just keep out of things that don't concern her?"

"Because it does concern her. You know, I've just about had it with you. Jim's right. You're nothing more than a spoilt brat. You're rude and totally inconsiderate of other people's feelings. You show no gratitude for what people do for you. The doctors here worked extremely hard to save your life, actually revived you several times, and this is how you repay them. You don't even value your own life."

Lou rolled her eyes. "You brought me here when I was dying—"

Jack shook his head. "You are *not* dying! The IV of antibiotics will deal with any residual infection. Your life isn't over. It's just changed. You just need time to adjust and learn to do things a little differently now, that's all."

"I know that now. Dr. Andrews told me, hours after I wrote that stupid letter. Then she made me go for a walk before I had a chance to throw it away." Lou folded her arms across her chest defensively. "And I tried to tell you earlier, but you said, and I quote, '*I don't want to hear it.*'"

Jack raised an eyebrow at her poor American accent. "Really?"

"Yes, really." She nodded. "You were too busy yelling at me and insisting that poor airman go write a report because he was in trouble for gossiping. You just assumed I was running away again."

"Weren't you?"

"No, actually I wasn't. I was trying to see if I could push the wretched chair by myself. Dr. Andrews was going on and on about me being independent, so I figured I'd try it. Show her when I got back inside. But the stupid chair doesn't have a reverse gear on it, so I was trying to find someplace to do a three-point turn. Only my hand got stuck and I tore out the IV somehow, and when I bent down to pick it up, the stupid chair overbalanced and I fell. Then you came and..." She shrugged.

"Why didn't you ask Airman Ryder to go with you? He would have helped."

"He was busy talking, and I didn't want to disturb him. Bad enough I'm stuck in here without being totally dependent on everyone for everything." She sighed. "And asking for help kind of defeats the 'getting you independent' bit she keeps going on about."

"Oh, honey," Jack said. "It's early days yet. We're here to help as much as we can, but you have to let us show you how to do these things before you can begin to master them. You're not on your own, no matter how much it feels like it."

Lou took a deep breath. Maybe he'd listen without condemning her. "It's bad, Jack. There's darkness everywhere. There is no way out. I can't do this. Don't you sit there and judge me either. You don't know what it's like to have everything taken away from you. To no longer be able to do things without help—simple things like going to the bathroom are impossible now. So don't you dare sit there and tell me how I should feel, because you don't know or understand how bad life gets. Or what it's like to know you must have done something really bad, because God obviously hates you so much that He did this to you."

Jack stood up and shoved his hands into his

pockets. "There you go again. That's just plain rude. You want to know what bad really is? Bad is sitting on a hillside in the Gulf after being shot down, holding your best friend in your arms. Watching him bleed to death from a massive head wound, while waiting for the rescue choppers, which never came in time. It took Will two hours to die. All I could do was hold him in my arms and tell him help was coming. Wars may change, but the pain of losing a friend never does. Or family."

Lou swallowed hard. "Family?" she asked.

Something dark shone in Jack's eyes for an instant before he continued. "My son, Billy. He was a cute little guy with blond hair—looked like his mom. He came home from school one day complaining he didn't feel well. He said the light hurt his eyes and that his head ached. Erin put him to bed. When I got home from work, he was still complaining his head hurt. That night, he started being sick."

He paused and gazed out of the window. "We dialed 9-1-1 and they rushed him to hospital. He was unconscious by the time we got there. They said he had meningitis. He died in my arms a few hours later." He whirled round and looked at her. His eyes glistened with tears. "Billy was seven when God took him. He'll never have the chances you've got. He'll never see another sunset or rainbow, never hear the birds sing or the waves crashing on the shore. He'll never go swimming or throw snowballs. There isn't a day goes by when I don't miss him."

He crossed the room and sat on the bed. He grabbed her hands. "I would give anything to have him back. Even in a wheelchair. I blamed God for taking him, the doctors for not saving him, Erin for not calling them or me sooner, me for not being there. But it was no one's fault. Not mine, not Erin's, not the doctors, and not God's."

"Who's Erin?"

"She was my wife. After Billy died, she wanted a divorce. She said there was nothing to keep us together anymore, that a fresh start would be the best thing for the both of us. We argued. She slammed out of the house and drove the car over a cliff. Deliberately, the police think, because there weren't any skid marks, and there weren't any other vehicles involved. If we hadn't argued, then maybe..." His voice caught and he paused.

He rubbed his hands over his face. "So I do know what it's like to be stuck in the darkness, Lou. I've been there for a long time. I spent hours going over that final conversation with Erin, before she killed herself. Were there any warning signs? Did I miss something? Could I have stopped her? It's the people left behind that pay the price. Trust me on that. I thought my life ended when Billy and Erin died. I had to bury my wife and son within two weeks of each other. I live with the regrets every day. And your mom knows what it's like as well. She was a mess after you and the others left."

Lou pointed to her legs. "What about this?"

"What about it? Seems to me you're more scared of what could happen now, rather than the actual injury itself."

She caught her breath. He was spot on there. "A little," she said, downplaying it.

"Only a little? What are you scared of? Being laughed at? Ignored? Teased? What?"

Lou shrugged. "Not being me. I'm not normal anymore. I want to be able to run and walk and do things for myself. When I want to do them, not when someone has a spare five minutes to fit me in. And I'd got my life mapped out. I can't exactly be the next great archaeologist now, can I?"

Jack rolled his eyes at her bad pun, then took her hand. "Lou, honey. Like I said earlier, it's early days yet. You gotta give yourself time to adjust, just like anyone does after losing a limb. This chair will make a huge difference. We can teach you easily how to get in and out of it. How to get into the bathroom and so on."

Lou picked at a nail. "I know being in a military hospital, they're used to this kind of injury, but..."

"Everyone feels like you do at first. Happy to be alive, but mourning the loss of part of them. It's a normal, healthy reaction."

"Are you sure?" she whispered.

"Yes. But this isn't the end of the road. It's just the start. There are other options once you're a little stronger. Doc Andrews said you could walk again."

"You mean crutches again? Or they'll give me a wooden leg?"

"Oh man, you missed your chance. We were going to have you fitted with a peg leg, eye patch, and stuffed parrot and turn you into a pirate." He grinned as she pulled a face at him. "Seriously, prosthetic limbs are slightly more sophisticated these days."

"Like what?"

"Like this." Jack lifted the leg of his uniform.

Her eyes widened at Jack's leg. Wow, he could run and everything. She'd never have guessed in a million years that he only had one leg. "How did you lose it? If you don't mind me asking?"

"Chopper crash soon after basic training. Once I was out of rehab, I was back at work, determined to learn how to fly choppers so no one could ever crash one on me again." Jack smiled. "You'll be able to be that famous archaeologist or win your Olympic medal yet. You'll see the sun rise and build snowmen. You can do all that in a wheelchair, never mind with a new leg. Don't give up."

"May as well. I've hurt too many people and now God is punishing me for it."

Jack sighed. "No, He's not. God doesn't do that. He loves us too much for that. Lou, you can't just give up. You have to fight."

"Already lost that fight."

"No, you haven't. You just need a little help. It's not failure to admit you can't cope. All you have to do is ask." He glanced at his watch, stood up, and went behind the chair.

"Jim told me that once."

"Then take it from the both of us."

"Where are we going?" Lou asked as he pulled her backward into the corridor. He locked the door and swung her round.

"Back to the infirmary because it's almost 1530," he answered. "I want you to do some serious thinking when we get there. I'll come by and see you later. You can't decide to do this for me or for your mom. You have to do it for yourself."

They crossed the car park. It was overcast and getting dark. It was also trying to rain. Almost as if the weather were mimicking the storm inside her. Lou glanced over her shoulder. "What do I do, Jack?"

"I can't tell you that. You either fight or you give in. Giving in means a feeding tube or the psych ward...or both, depending on Doc Andrews. Though she may relent when you explain to her that you weren't doing a runner or trying to kill yourself. However, either way, it's your choice. There are people here who love you very much and would miss you terribly if you weren't here. They may not show it as much or as often as you need, but they care very much about what happens to you."

The guard on the main door opened it for them. Jack pushed her to the lifts. He pressed the call button. "And I'll tell you something else. You're not alone." The lift came and he pushed her inside. He hit the floor button. "It may feel like you're the only person for miles, but I can assure you that you're not. If you want help, or just someone to talk to or a shoulder to cry on, I'm here. All you have to do is ask. It's not a crime to admit you need someone now and again. And another thing. God doesn't hate you."

The lift doors opened and they went down the corridor in silence. Jack backed through the infirmary doors and pushed her across to her bed. He lifted her onto the bed and pulled up the covers. "Want to sit up or lie down?"

"Lying down sounds good. Been sat up for hours and I'm not used to it."

He winked. "Getting soft spending far too much time in bed. We'll have to change that. I'll come back and see you after dinner."

She nodded, glad to be lying down again. "Will you be on your own?"

"If that's what you want."

"Yes, it is." Lou caught his arm and looked at him. "Jack."

"Yes?"

"Help me please. I can't do it on my own."

"I'll help. You do some thinking while I'm gone.

And eat something."

"Aye, sir."

No sooner had Jack left, than General Merrick came over and sat beside her. "I heard about your escape attempt," she began firmly.

"I wasn't..." Lou began, but at the look in the general's eye, she was tempted to shut up. Sometimes not saying anything was the best option. But let's face it, she'd gotten Airman Ryder into hot water and it wasn't fair he should be in trouble because of her. She explained her side of things quietly.

General Merrick listened and then began speaking just as quietly.

Usually Lou would have switched off, but Jack's words had woken something within her. So for one of the few times in her life, she really listened. Her face burned and her stomach churned.

"You now have an escort—Sergeant Whitlock," the general finished. "She will not let you out of her sight."

After General Merrick left and Sergeant Whitlock took up post by the door, Lou lay back on her pillows deep in thought. *I made a mistake and I'm paying the price for it now. If I leave, then other people will pay the price.* She finally understood what Jack had told her all those weeks ago. *Grief is the price you pay for love.* So many things had happened because of the decisions she had made. So many people hurt, so many lives altered because of her. Once more, the cloud descended, but this time, she knew that help was only a shout away.

14

An hour later, Dr. Andrews crossed the infirmary to Lou. "How are you doing?" she asked.

"I could do with a couple of codeine tablets," Lou said. "Please," she added.

"I think I can go stronger than codeine. Would you like some dinner?"

"Jack already made me eat lunch."

"Lunch was hours ago. Wanna try that one again? I have a nice feeding tube with your name on it otherwise. It doesn't have to be much, just a little."

Lou sucked in a deep breath. "Chips, if they have them—or fries or whatever you call them. And I'd love a cup of tea. That one earlier was nice."

Dr. Andrews smiled. "I'll see what I can do. Let's sit you up a bit."

"Thank you." She leaned against the pillows as the head of the bed raised her upwards.

"I won't be long."

Lou watched her go. She glanced down at her legs—well, leg and a half. It was weird. She could still feel it. Half the pain she felt was from the limb that wasn't there. And her toes still itched. The pain was real enough; just there was no reason for it. She turned her thoughts to what Jack had said. He made a lot of sense for a grown-up, she decided.

Dr. Andrews came back with a tray of food and a syringe. "One mug of tea, along with sausages, peas, and fries."

"Peas are evil," Lou told her. "Little green balls of pure nastiness."

"So don't eat the peas." She put the tray on the table and injected the morphine into the cannula. "It should start to work soon," she said, pulling the table across the bed. "I'll set the morphine pump up again in a while. Jim's here to see you if you feel up to it."

Lou nodded, not minding the fact there was more on the plate than she'd asked for. "Sure. So long as I can eat at the same time."

Dr. Andrews said, "Don't see why not." She left Lou and beckoned Jim over.

Jim came across and sat by the bed. "Those chips smell good," he said. "Can I have one?"

"Are you here for the chips or me?" Lou asked.

He thought for a minute. "Lou or chips? Lou. Chips. Difficult one. Um...the chips."

"That's what I thought. Help yourself. And you can have *all* the peas."

Jim took one of the chips and ate it slowly.

"How was the beach?" Lou asked. She stabbed one of the sausages with the fork and bit into it.

Jim smiled. "Your mum is brilliant at beach volleyball. We beat the pants off the other team, thanks to her. How was your day?"

Lou shrugged. "It went. Jim, can I ask you something?"

"Sure," he replied, taking another chip.

"Am I a particularly bad person? I mean, is God punishing me for running away?"

Jim looked at her curiously. "Because you lost your leg?"

"Amongst other things. Have the other sausage,

because I won't eat it."

"OK, thanks." He took the sausage. "And to answer your question, no," Jim replied emphatically, shaking his head. "God doesn't work like that. He loves you. He wouldn't take away your leg to punish you. Any more than my parents being caught in the tsunami or your dad being killed or Deefer dying was a punishment either. God may have allowed the injury to get your attention, but He certainly isn't punishing you."

Lou finished the chips. "But how do I know He loves me?"

"Because He sent His only Son, Jesus, to die for you."

Lou looked at Jim. "If He loves me that much, then why did this happen? How can a God who loves me, this great, loving, and good God, do this? Was He asleep? Busy elsewhere?"

"Lou, God never sleeps. He is always watching over you. Psalm 139:2–4 says so. He always does what is best for you. He knows what is good for you and that is what He does. Even though it may not seem like it at the time."

Lou snorted. "Hah. You got that right."

Jim looked at her. "Lou. God does love you. He knows how you feel."

"Prove it. Prove that He loves me. Prove to me He knows what I'm feeling." She broke off and looked up as Jack came across.

"Hi," he said. "Am I interrupting?"

"No," Jim said, noticing the Bible that Jack was carrying. "Maybe you're just the person we need. Lou wants proof that God loves her and knows how she feels."

Clare Revell

Jack looked at Lou.

She looked at him then down at the plate. "I just can't get past the fact that He could let this happen if He isn't picking on me. Or other bad stuff. If God is really out there..."

"Oh, God is out there, Lou," Jack said. "And He knows how you feel." He moved the table out of the way and sat next to her on the bed. He handed Lou his Bible. "Psalm 88," he said. "Read it and then tell me that God doesn't know how you feel."

Lou flicked through it and found it.

"Read it aloud," Jack told her.

"I am overwhelmed with troubles and my life draws near to death. I am counted among those who go down to the pit; I am like one without strength. I am set apart with the dead, like the slain who lie in the grave, whom You remember no more, who are cut off from Your care. You have put me in the lowest pit, in the darkest depths. Your wrath lies heavily on me; You have overwhelmed me with all Your waves. You have taken from me my closest friends and have made me repulsive to them. I am confined and cannot escape; my eyes are dim with grief. I call to You, Lord, every day; I spread out my hands to You—"

As she read, her voice wavered and tears blurred her vision. She struggled on, but eventually her voice broke.

Jack took the Bible from her and continued to read from verse thirteen. *"But I cry to You for help, Lord; in the morning my prayer comes before You. Why, Lord, do You reject me and hide Your face from me? From my youth I have suffered and been close to death; I have borne Your terrors and am in despair. Your wrath has swept over me; Your terrors have destroyed me. All day long they surround me like a flood; they have completely engulfed me. You have taken from me friend and neighbor—darkness is my closest friend."*

Jack stopped reading. The silence was only broken by Lou's sobs. He put the Bible down and took her in his arms. "You see, even God knows where you are coming from. Jesus Himself felt alone and separated from God. Remember how, on the cross, He quoted Psalm twenty-two, *'My God, My God, why have You forsaken Me?'"*

Jim reread part of Psalm 88:8. *"You have taken from me my closest friends and have made me repulsive to them."*

"I've managed that one," Lou sobbed. "Haven't I?"

"You tried," Jim agreed.

She glanced up at him.

"But it'll take way more than one of your bad moods to get rid of us. You see, we love you and don't like to see you unhappy. When you're sad, it makes us sad, too."

Jack held her tightly, her tears soaking his shirt. "And God loves you, too. John three sixteen says so."

"I know that one," Lou said quietly.

"I guess you know Psalm twenty-three?" Jack asked.

She nodded. *"The Lord is my shepherd."*

Jack smiled. "My pastor always says that goodness and mercy are the sheepdogs."

She frowned. "Sheepdogs?"

"Jesus is the shepherd, I'm the sheep, and if goodness and mercy follow me, then that makes them…"

"Sheepdogs. I get it. That's clever."

"What about Malachi four verse two?"

Lou shook her head. "No. Never been one for

reading the Bible. Couldn't even tell you where that book is."

"*But for you who revere My name, the sun of righteousness will rise with healing in its rays. And you will go out and frolic like well-fed calves*," Jim read.

"Can't leap anywhere, can I? I can't even walk," she sighed.

"It doesn't just mean literally leap," Jack explained. "God leads us from darkness into light, sickness to health, bondage to freedom, cold to warmth, stuntedness to growth, inactivity to usefulness, and joylessness to joy. Because He loves you."

Lou shook her head. "Not me. I'm not good enough."

"Especially you," Jack told her. "In Matthew nine verse thirteen Jesus says, '*For I have not come to call the righteous, but sinners.*" He looked across at Jim. "There's a list in the front of my Bible. Would you read them please?"

Jim nodded. He pulled out the piece of paper and looked at it. "Fourteen of them," he said. "Do you want me to read them all?"

"Leave the last one for now."

Jim opened the Bible and read Jack's list. As he read, Lou's sobs diminished, and she listened, really listened.

When he finished, Lou looked at Jack. "But will God want me? I mean, what good am I to anyone now?"

Jack smiled. "Lou, do you know the story of the prodigal son?"

"Yeah. He ran away and spent all his father's money."

"When he came home, did his father yell at him or refuse to let him back in the house?"

"No."

Jack said, "He ran to his son. He came to him, met him on the road, even though the son had hurt him badly by running away and disobeying him. Then he threw a huge party for him because the son he thought was dead was alive and had come home. He never stopped loving him. Your mom still loves you, doesn't she, even though you ran away?"

"She says she does."

Jack looked at her. "Your mom met you on the runway. According to General Merrick, she all but ran out there as soon as she knew your chopper was inbound. She's living on the base, hardly left your side the first couple of days, unless the doc threw her out or I made her lie down and sleep. Now if that's not love, then I don't know what is."

Lou looked at him in amazement. "Even after I was horrid to her?"

"Especially after you were horrid to her. Likewise, your Heavenly Father loves you. Why should He turn His back on you now?"

"Yeah, but I've done religion all my life. It doesn't mean anything. You're different though, Jack. Despite everything you told me earlier about your wife and son and your leg, you still believe in a loving God. You talk like it means something, like Jesus is real to you. Like you have hope. Where is this hope?"

Jack looked down at her. "To put it simply," he began, "there is only one hope—Jesus. God loves you with an everlasting love. We're not just flesh and blood, we have a soul. But unlike our body, the soul is eternal. God made it like that because He wants a relationship with us. Not just for the few years we are on the earth, but forever." Lou glanced at Jim. He nodded, agreeing with what Jack was saying.

Jack continued, "Jesus loves you. He loved you enough to die on the cross to pay the price of your sins for you. There is nothing you have done nor can ever do that will stop Him from loving you or wanting a permanent relationship with you. But it has to be all or nothing. No half measures. He wants all of you, all the time. A daily two-way relationship. He's waiting for you now."

She frowned. "It can't be that easy, surely?"

"Yes and no," Jack said. "Life isn't easy. There is no magic cure. I still have bad days now when I miss Billy and Erin, or have flashbacks about Will, but I have God to get me through them. He'll do the same for you if you ask."

Lou looked at him. "I want that for myself," she said.

Jack nodded. "Let's pray," he said. He led them in prayer.

Jim joined in.

Then Lou, stumbling over her words and interspaced with sobs, confessed her sins and accepted Jesus as her Lord and Savior. Afterwards she looked up at Jack, a sense of peace flooding her heart and mind. It was as if the clouds were beginning to break— a tiny ray of hope peeping through on a stormy day.

15

Lou looked up as Jack finished praying. "Thank you, Jack."

He hugged her tightly and leant her back against the pillows. "It's not gonna be easy," he told her. "You need to work hard at it. Read the Bible and pray every day. At least once."

"I realize that," Lou said. "I don't have a Bible though."

"There is a Gideon New Testament in the drawer next to you. It's got suggested readings in the front of it. It'll do until you get one of your own." He smiled at her. "You'll also need to work on your physio and follow the doc's instructions to the letter. If you want this prosthesis, you have to earn it and learn to walk again. I'll be here though, every step of the way."

Lou nodded then groaned. "Your jokes are as bad as Jim's."

Jack looked surprised. "Joke?" he queried.

"Prosthesis…learning to walk again…every 'step' of the way," Lou said.

Jack grinned. "You ain't seen nothing yet, kid. There's a whole lot more where that came from. And get used to it. Because as long as your mom wants me around, you get me too."

Lou grinned back. "Oh joy." She glanced across at the table. "I suppose the tea is cold."

"As it should be." Jack winked.

Lou pulled a face. "No, tea is hot. With milk and sugar in it."

"I'll get you another," Jim said. He looked across at Jack. "Thank you," he said.

"It's what friends are for." Jack smiled.

"You've gone above and beyond that today," Jim told him. He looked at Lou. "Do you want anything else or just the tea?"

"Can you ask if the others can come in for a bit? I've pushed them away for too long. We could teach Jack how to play Phase 10. But I'd like to see Mum first."

"I'll ask. The doc might want you to rest though, but I'll go ask."

Lou watched as Jim went over to Dr. Andrews's office and spoke to her. He shot her a thumbs-up across the ward and left. Lou looked at Jack. "About this morning," she began. "I really wasn't trying to run..."

"It's forgotten. Let's just move on."

"OK. Thank you. Airman Ryder isn't in too much trouble, is he?"

"No," Jack said. "I dealt with it."

Dr. Andrews came over. "How are you feeling?" she asked, shoving a thermometer in Lou's mouth and taking hold of her wrist.

Lou grinned. "How do I answer with this in my mouth?"

"Ack, don't talk with your mouth full," Jack said. "It's rude."

"Sorry, *Uncle* Jack."

"And stop with the uncle."

Dr. Andrews removed the thermometer and read it. "Normal," she said. "So's your pulse. Are you up to more visitors? You've had a busy day."

"I've shut them out for too long," Lou said. "What time is it?"

"1945. Not too late." She jotted things down on the chart and hung it back up. "OK, they can visit for a while, but I don't want them staying too late."

Mum came across, carrying a tray of tea. "I brought three," she said. "Figured Jack might want one."

"Only if his is cold," Lou said quickly.

Jack rolled his eyes. "Thanks, Nicky, but I was going to leave you ladies to it."

Lou shook her head. "You don't have to go, Jack." She held out her arms to her mother.

Mum put the tray down and wrapped her arms tightly around Lou.

Lou hugged her tightly, crying hard. "I'm sorry. I hurt you so much. I can never make it up to you."

Mum hugged her back. "You don't have to. You're my daughter. I will always love you. No matter what. Jack told me how down you'd felt. Why didn't you tell me things were that bad?"

"I couldn't. There was no one I felt I could trust. And after Jack dragged me to the canteen to make me eat, I hated him." She looked at Jack. "You knew how I felt about things, but ignored my wishes. That's why I couldn't tell anyone at all, because you grown-ups just wouldn't understand. I didn't understand my feelings myself. So I couldn't explain them even if I could find the words or someone I thought I could trust. All I knew was that I'd had enough and felt you'd be better off without me."

"I'd never be better off without you," Mum told her. "I love you."

"I know that now." Lou glanced over at Jack. "But I don't hate you anymore, Jack."

"Glad to hear it," Jack said quietly.

"I'm sorry I ever felt that way. You did me a favor, even though I didn't see it at the time. I owe you one. You saved my life in lots of ways."

Mum said, "Promise me you will talk to someone."

"I start counseling tomorrow," Lou said. "General Merrick gave me no choice." She smiled at Jack over Mum's shoulder. "But I would have done it anyway. A friend suggested it. Well, *Uncle* Jack…"

Jack rolled his eyes, trying to look fierce, but his chuckle gave him away. "I have asked you repeatedly *not* to call me uncle, kid." He handed her one of the mugs. "So, are you going to come to church with us on Sunday, assuming I can sneak you past that guard dog of a doc over there?"

"Guard dog?" Lou frowned slightly, then the penny dropped. "Oh, yeah, she said you were a horrid patient who did anything he could to avoid seeing her."

"Did she now?"

"Quite funny actually. Big guy like you afraid of a little woman like her."

Jack laughed. "Don't let her hear you say that. Besides, she has a large assortment of very big needles."

Lou nodded. "And feeding tubes, apparently."

Mum laughed with them. "Why church? You said church wasn't your cup of tea and you wouldn't go if I paid you. Unless Jim went, then you'd go."

Lou smiled. "That's something else that Jack did. He helped God find me."

Jack shook his head. "God knew where you were all along, kid. I just gave you a shove in His direction."

Mum hugged Lou again, taking care not to spill the tea. "That's wonderful, sweetheart. I'll have to buy you a Bible, because I don't suppose you kept yours."

Lou shook her head. "Maybe you and Jack could choose one together," she said.

Jack took hold of her mum's hand. "We'd like that."

Jim tapped on the door. Jack beckoned him in. He nodded and came in, followed by Staci, Ailsa, and his parents. With the ever-present Sergeant Peterson and Staff Sergeant Chaney close behind.

Lou hugged Bill and Di, not having seen them since she'd gotten onto the base. She chatted with them for a few minutes, then looked at the others. It still amazed her that they wanted anything to do with her. But then love didn't ask questions. It was just there.

"So who's that on the door?" Staci asked, tossing the cards onto the table by Lou's bed.

Lou looked up. "That's Sergeant Whitlock, my escort."

"You have an escort now?" Ailsa said. "What did you do?"

Lou shrugged. "I just decided that if you can't beat them, join them. Why should you guys have all the fun? Besides, if my escort is going to follow me everywhere, then she can push the wheelchair."

Jim shook his head and laughed. "You are a card, you know that?"

Lou poked out her tongue at him. "Actually, these are cards. I'm a person." She waved the pack at him before turning out all the cards and shuffling them.

Jim groaned. "Jack, we unleashed a monster," he

said in a stage whisper. "She found her sense of humor."

Staci played along, throwing her hands up in horror. "Oh no, not her sense of humor. I thought you'd thrown that overboard along with the phone."

"It was in with the logbook," Lou told them. "Page forty-seven, paragraph three, line six..." She broke off as Jim tossed a pillow at her. She caught it and tossed it back. "So are we playing cards or just trading insults all night?"

Jim grinned. "I can multitask and do both."

"Rubbish," Staci said. "You're a man. You can't multitask." She got up and, with Ailsa's help, pulled over all the tables she could find and put them together over Lou's bed.

Sergeant Peterson and Staff Sergeant Chaney sat over with Sergeant Whitlock by the door.

Lou glanced at them and then looked at Jim. "No one is gonna go anywhere tonight," she deadpanned.

"Just pretend they're keeping someone out rather than us inside," Jim laughed.

"Sounds good to me." Lou dealt the cards. She picked hers up and explained the rules to Jack. She glared at her cards. How was she supposed to do two sets of three with ten cards where no two numbers were the same? "Nothing changes," she said.

After a couple of hours, Dr. Andrews announced the end of visiting time. She chased the others out. Mum and Jack stood to go with them.

Lou said, "Mum?"

Mum turned. "Yes, love?"

"What's going to happen now?"

"With what?"

"Ailsa, for one thing."

Mum looked at Jack. "I'll catch you up. Wait for me in the mess." As he nodded and headed out, she sat down on the bed. "Well, Bill and Di have said that Ailsa can live with them if she wants to. She's eighteen, so she won't have to go into foster care or into the system at all. They'll tell the authorities she's not dead, get her passport sorted with the embassy here. Then they'll go back to England."

"Go back to England?" Lou's stomach fell. "Jim and Staci too?"

Mum smiled. "Of course. They'll live with their parents until they go back onto the mission field. Di is talking about taking Staci with them next time. It'll be up to Jim if he goes with them. And that depends on if he has a job and where he's working."

Tears burned Lou's eyes, irritating her. "I don't want them to go."

"Sweetheart, there isn't anything we can do about it. You know them staying with us was only temporary."

"Are we going back with them?"

"Jack's asked me to stay here. And for the moment, that's probably for the best." She held up a hand as Lou started to object. "While you're in here and being treated..."

"Can't they do that at home?"

"We don't have a home," Mum said. "I told you that already."

"Oh, right...yeah." She sucked in a deep breath. "So that's it then. They go back to England and I...I'm alone again."

Mum's fingers were warm against Lou's face as she tucked her hair behind her ears. "No, honey, you're not alone. Not anymore."

16

February 15.

Lou looked up at Jim and Staci. "So, this is it then? You're really leaving?" She looked at the clock. "Only I thought the flight left at two?"

Jim nodded. "Yeah, it does, but we have to drive to the airport. It's a two-hour check-in so...yeah, we're going now. As the song says, '*All my bags are packed; I'm ready to go. I'm standing here outside your door.*' Well, next to your bed to be precise."

"I don't want you to go." She looked at him. Tears filled her eyes. "Tell them you won't go."

"We have to," he said. "Us staying with you was only while Mum and Dad were away, you know that."

"But we've been together for months," she whispered. "You've been there all day every day since June. Well, longer than that. Since Bill and Di left in March of last year."

Jim nodded. "Yeah."

Staci picked at a nail. "Ailsa is coming with us. She and Jim are officially going out now, not that they'll admit it. As much as I don't want to go, it'll be nice to be home again. And a new home, too. I get first choice of the bedrooms."

Jim pulled her hair. "No, you don't, kiddo. I'm oldest; I get first pick."

"Mum said I do," Staci insisted. "Anyway, it's

ladies first. You get the leftovers."

Jim rolled his eyes. "Fine, I'll sleep up on the roof with the cats, as Aunt Edith always used to say." He looked at Lou. "But we'll write, and message and video call you." He hugged her. "You take care and do what the doctor says."

She nodded slowly. She hugged Staci and watched as they headed across the room to where Bill and Di waited. Her heart broke as their footsteps got farther and farther away.

Tears rolling down her face, she pulled herself from the bed to the chair and grabbed the wheels. Frustration mounted as the chair remained stuck between the bed and the cupboard. "Come on," she hissed.

"Lou? Where are you going?" Jack asked.

"Doesn't matter," she whispered. "They've gone. And it's just me now."

"Not so," he said gently. "It just so happens that I have the rest of the day off. And it's your mom's birthday on Saturday, isn't it?"

Lou took the tissue he offered and blotted her eyes with it. "Yeah."

"So, I thought, if you put some clothes on, rather than those pyjamas you've been living in the past couple of weeks, we could hit the shops. Buy her something nice."

"I don't have any money…"

Jack winked. "I have it on good authority that you have several months' worth allowance owing you."

"And I don't have any clothes either."

He held out a bag. "How's this?"

Lou looked in the bag. "Jack?"

"I lived in sweatpants after they took my leg," he

said. "We fold the extra fabric up and you sit on it for now. Once you get your new leg, just wear them as normal. And if you change quickly, we can sneak out before Dragon Doc comes on duty."

"But everyone will notice my leg isn't there."

Jack rolled his eyes. "This is an Air Force base. We get wounded airmen here all the time. Arms and legs in casts or missing. No one is going to notice, unless you go out there with nothing on. And it's a bit damp for that, as it rained this morning. Now hurry up or she'll be here and we won't be going anywhere."

"OK."

Jack nodded and pulled the curtains around the bed.

Lou changed quickly. "OK."

Jack opened the curtains and looked at her. "Actually, where's your other shoe?"

"Under the bed. Don't need it."

He grinned. "Yes, we do." He pulled the empty trouser leg free and shoved it inside her shoe. He fastened the two together with a lace and grinned. "Perfect."

Lou looked down at her feet. "Thank you."

"You're welcome. Now we gotta dash."

Dr. Andrews rounded the corner just as they reached the ward door. "Colonel? Lou? What are you doing?"

"Just passing—" He paused as a voice echoed over the Tannoy.

"Dr. Andrews to main reception. Dr. Andrews to main reception."

Dr. Andrews looked at them. "I'll be back."

"See ya, Doc." Jack waved as she ran off then winked at Lou.

"What's so funny?"

"Ed promised a distraction if we got caught. We've got about ten minutes to get out of here. Then an hour or so to shop before your mom meets us for coffee. Then we're sneaking back in here before she notices."

Lou sniffled again. Sneaking out wasn't half as much fun on her own. Last time she'd sneaked off, Jim and Staci had been with her.

Jack dropped another tissue on her lap. "And if you're good," he added as he sped down the corridor towards the lifts, "tomorrow we'll go check out my place and you can decide if you want the green room or the yellow room as yours."

Despite the ache filling her and the incredible sense of loneliness, Lou enjoyed shopping with Jack. He insisted on modeling the shirts she was looking at, or the bracelets or necklaces, even the scarfs.

"Which is it going to be?" Jack asked.

"I don't know," she said. "The scarf and the bracelet are both pretty, but the bracelet is way more than I can afford." She looked at them. "The scarf."

Jack hunkered down next to the chair. "Don't worry about the cost. How about we get both? We could even get *Mom* engraved on it if you like."

Lou looked at him. "*Mum,*" she corrected. "It's *English.*"

Jack winked. "You Brits never could spell. Let's go and pay and then go and find her. I'll pop back and pick the bracelet up in a few."

"Won't she get suspicious?"

Jack shook his head. "Nah, she'll be too busy sharing one of those massive coconut-and-pineapple ice creams with you."

Lou's eyes widened. "I thought Staci was kidding about those."

"Nope. Let's go."

****

Lou sat next to Mum sharing the ice cream. Jack had vanished on the pretext of finding a men's room. Lou looked at the spoon in her hand. "Miss them," she said.

Mum nodded. "Yeah. The house will be a lot quieter without them. But you should be able to come home soon."

"Jack said he'd sneak me out again tomorrow so I could pick a bedroom. Either the green or yellow one."

Mum looked at her, then at the ice cream. "Well, the green room is pretty, looks over the front of the house. But the yellow room has an en-suite bathroom. Both are upstairs, but Jack was talking about converting the dining room into a bedroom for you to begin with. Until you can master the stairs, which he reckons will take less than a week."

"Seriously?"

Mum winked. "Apparently it took him a month to do stairs, but he says you're way more stubborn than he is and will do it in a week. Especially if you get told not to do it."

Lou licked the spoon clean. "I did the ones on the boat as soon as I got out of bed. Mind you, I kind of had to."

"Oh, and we thought we'd take you clothes shopping off base tomorrow as well. Figured you could do with a whole new wardrobe."

Jack came back over with a carrier bag in his hand.

"I picked up a few things on my way back from the men's room."

Mum raised an eyebrow. "Really?"

He nodded. "As Lou's gonna be able to use the shower later, I thought she might like some nice shower gel. And now we really ought to get back before the doc notices."

Lou took the bag and held it as Jack pushed her back to the infirmary. She had no idea how he expected no one to notice she'd gone.

Jack slowed down as he reached Dr. Andrews's office, then sped up, running past it, before he slowed again, whistling innocently.

"Colonel?"

Lou caught her breath. "Here we go…"

Jack turned. "Yes, Doc?"

"Please sign her out the next time you decide to go for a walk. I don't want to have to report her or you AWOL."

Lou snorted, turning it into a cough.

"Now get her into bed before that cough gets any worse."

Jack grinned. "Yes, ma'am."

As he pushed her down the corridor, Lou was convinced she heard laughter coming from the doctor's office.

17

Six Months Later, July 10.

The phone rang. "Want me to get it?" Lou asked. She, Jim, and her mum had flown to the UK to pick up Staci for the summer holidays, as Bill and Di were off to a missionary convention. Staci was living with her parents in England while they were on sabbatical.

Jim and Ailsa were staying at Jack's place on Guam. Like Jack had originally said, there was plenty of room, and both Jim and Ailsa were spending a lot of time helping with her physio.

Jim grinned. "Go for it. We know who it's going to be anyway."

"Well, one of two people by my count." She crossed the living room of Bill and Di's house in Southampton, England, and grabbed the phone before it had rung three times. "Kirk residence, hello? Hi, Jack. Yeah, I'll get her for you." She tossed the cordless phone to her mum. "It's for you-ou."

Mum smiled. "Thanks."

Lou went back across to the others. She was almost used to the prosthesis now, but very self-conscious about it, choosing to wear trousers rather than skirts. "That's the third time Jack's rung today. I think he misses her."

Jim grinned at her. "You'll be in love yourself one day. Then you'll understand."

"Aw. Missing Ailsa, are we?" Lou teased.

Jim blushed.

Staci laughed. "That'll be a yes then," she said. She laid down her cards. "Out."

"Well done, kiddo," Jim said, counting his cards. "Fifteen. Doesn't seem possible that it's been thirteen months since we left to find Mum and Dad, does it?"

"Was it really?" Lou asked, pulling a face at her cards. "One hundred and five."

"Yeah. It's July 10. This time last year, we were recovering from Erika. Nichola's got eighty-five."

Mum put the phone down. "Right. Are you lot ready to go?"

"Yes," they answered in unison.

"How's Ailsa?" Jim asked.

"She's fine. Jack says she would say hi, but she's in bed. It's late over there."

"They are nine hours ahead. It's 2 PM here, so it must be 11 PM over there," Lou said. "Jack ringing to say good night?"

"He's on duty. He and Ailsa are staying at the base while he's on nights. It's the last one tonight."

Jim looked thoughtful. "Night flying must be well cool," he said wistfully.

"Cool?" Lou said. "Cool? You've been hanging round Jack for too long."

Jim threw a cushion at her. "You can talk. You spend more time with him than anyone, except your mum."

"At least I don't come out with Jack-isms though."

"What about 'for crying out loud' then?"

"Yeah, well. Although I probably got that from you..." She broke off laughing as Jim launched an all-out cushion assault. She begged for mercy and Jim reluctantly accepted.

"What I would give to join the Air Force and do it."

"Throw cushions at people and get paid for it?" Lou asked, grinning at him.

"No, go night flying, silly. I'm still hoping to hear from them soon."

"In your dreams, mate," Staci said. "There is no way the US Air Force would have you. You're British, for a start."

He looked at Staci. "If not, then I'll try the RAF, kiddo."

"And stop calling me kiddo. I'm fourteen now."

They all pulled on their jackets and Lou grabbed her crutches. She didn't yet trust her prosthesis enough to go out of the house without backup, as Jack termed it. They'd offered her a cane, but she'd pointed out she was a teenager, not an old granny lady. She followed the others to the front door.

Staci said, "So what's the plan of action for this afty?"

"I thought we'd go to the river," Mum said. "Then the cinema and pizza. Give your parents time to pack without your help."

"Sounds neat," Staci said.

Lou absently glanced over her shoulder as they reached the car. It was as if someone was missing, she just wasn't sure who.

They drove across town to Townhill Park and passed the block of flats Lou used to call home.

Lou looked out the window. "It hasn't changed. Look, there are the shops." They drove along the way they had walked so many times, Mum unknowingly going the same way Matt had taken them that last time.

In Riverside Park, Lou got out of the car and looked round for Deefer.

"He's not here, love," Mum said.

"I haven't done that in a long time," Lou said. "It's being back here. There are just so many memories."

They walked through the park towards the river. The river this time though was dull and grey, reflecting the thick cloud cover. Jim bounced stones off the surface. "It's a shame Ailsa couldn't come," he said. "I wanted to show her all this. Show her where it all began."

"You can come back," Lou said, looking round her. "She had to stay and study for those exams."

"She could have studied here," Jim objected.

"I don't think so," Staci said. "No one can study with you around, bro."

"Thanks for the vote of confidence, kiddo."

They reached the play area and Staci looked wistfully at the swings. "Please, Jim," she said. "I'm not much over twelve."

"You're fourteen, but go on then. I'll push you, as the park is empty." He opened the gate and followed her into the playground.

Lou watched as Jim pushed Staci on the swing, higher and higher, until she yelled, "I'm flying."

Lou absently looked down at her heels.

Mum looked sadly at her. "You miss him, don't you?"

Lou nodded. "Yes. More than I thought I would."

"Have you thought any more about getting another dog?"

"No. I could never replace Deefer."

"I wouldn't expect you to. Like I could never

replace your dad."

Lou looked at her mother. She had blossomed over the last few months. Not just because she had her family back, but as her relationship with Jack had grown. It had definitely been a good day when he had come into their lives. Even if it hadn't seemed like it that afternoon in Cornwall. She looked over at the others. "Come on," she called. "It's cold standing here."

Jim stopped the swing and Staci reluctantly got off. They came back through the gate to the others and set off under the bridge. The sign saying *Cobden Boat Hire* was more faded than it had been.

Matt saw them coming and went across to meet them. "Hello, stranger," he said, shaking Jim's hand. "How are you?"

"Good. You?"

"Yeah, good. I got your letter and I've been meaning to reply. But I've been rushed off my feet here, what with setting up the website and all. Sounds like quite an adventure you had."

Jim grinned. "Yeah, it was. A bit too exciting at times though."

"Exciting?" Staci exclaimed. "Scary, more like."

Matt smiled. "I can't stop to chat, I'm afraid. We have a big repair job on. I'll e-mail you and keep in touch that way."

Mum looked at her watch. "C'mon, we'd better get going if we are going to catch this film."

They walked back to the car in the deepening gloom, Lou saying goodbye to all the places that she had played in as a child and never expected to see again. Just before they got to the car, the heavens opened and the rain came down in torrents. They ran the rest of the way, getting soaked.

"Ugh," Lou said, climbing into the car and pushing her wet hair out of her eyes.

Mum said, "We don't have time to change. Do you mind staying wet?"

"No," said Staci. "I've waited years to hear that."

"Waited years to hear what?" Mum asked, starting the car.

"That I have to stay in my wet clothes." Staci laughed. The others joined in.

"I shan't make a habit of it though," Mum told them. "So make the most of it."

They drove towards the cinema, passing the school that Lou had attended. "Do you realize that they don't break up for another three weeks," she gloated.

The film was good, and when they came out, Mum smiled at them. "Who's hungry then?" she asked.

"Me."

"Anyone else except Staci?" Mum asked as everyone laughed.

****

The following day, their last before going home to Guam, was a Sunday. Jim was pleased that Lou was going to accompany them to church. He'd half expected her to have wavered in her faith without them around, but she hadn't. They went to the church they used to go to and sat in the same pew. They sang Jim's favorite hymn, "Amazing Grace."

After lunch they started packing. Lou took off the leg and hobbled round on her crutches. Nichola looked at her. "You have to persevere with it."

"I know, Mum. It's just uncomfortable today. I thought I might go for a swim in the pool over the road. Anyone coming?"

When no one answered, Jim said, "I'll come and time you if you like."

"Please." Lou grabbed her stuff.

"Any excuse not to pack," Nichola said, smiling.

"I'll do it later," Lou said.

"I'll do it now," Nichola replied. "Go on. Go swimming."

"Thanks, Mum." Lou kissed her and she and Jim headed for the pool.

Jim watched as Lou swam cleanly, smoothly, and quickly through the water, her right leg more than making up for the absence of the left. She hit the end of the pool and looked up at him. "Well?"

"Two whole seconds off your fastest time." He smiled. "Your coach will be impressed."

"He reckons I might be good enough for the Paralympics," Lou said proudly. "I may get my Olympic medal yet."

A figure came over to Jim as Lou set off down the pool again. "She's good," he said. "And fast."

Jim looked at the stranger. "She always has been a good swimmer. Even before she lost her leg."

"What happened, if you don't mind me asking?"

"Shark attack last year. Why?"

"She looks familiar. Of course, I only met this girl myself briefly and only the once, but I never forget a face. In my line of work you can't afford to." He leaned on his cane. "I was injured in an explosion at the docks last year. I was trapped underwater for what seemed like forever. I thought I was going to die, but a young girl saved me. She pulled me and two of my colleagues from the wreckage of the police boat."

Jim looked at him and felt a pang of guilt as he realized who this man was.

The man held out a hand. "Detective Inspector Steve Sutton."

Jim shook his hand. "Jim Kirk. The mermaid is my best friend—Lou Benson. She's the one who rescued you. I was so mad at her for doing so. No offense, but we were leaving the country to find my parents and she'd stowed away. I thought she was going to get us caught."

****

Lou reached the other end of the pool. She pulled herself up the steps and leant against the pool rail. She pulled on her toweling robe and slid her arms into her crutches. She looked at the man standing next to Jim. He looked familiar. She closed her eyes as a sudden flashback took her by surprise. Once again, she was under the water. A shark came rushing towards her. Flames surrounded her. A face under the water surrounded by wreckage.

"Lou?"

That was Jim's voice.

"Lou? Are you OK? There's someone wants to talk to you."

She opened her eyes and forced them to focus on Jim. "I'm fine," she said, to brush off the concern in his face. "Honestly."

"Are you sure?" He didn't sound convinced, but that was him all over.

She nodded. "So who wants to see me?"

"One of the blokes you rescued from that boat

explosion. Come on."

She nodded and gripped the crutches firmly before following Jim across the poolside to where the man waited.

****

Jim walked with her. For a minute she'd been someplace else. Jack had warned him to watch Lou for flashbacks and he was convinced she'd just had one, even if she hadn't said as much. Honestly, he was surprised she swam as much as she did. There was no way he was going to get back in the water any time soon, and he wasn't the one who'd been injured by the shark.

She held out her hand. "Lou Benson," she said.

"Detective Inspector Steve Sutton," he replied, shaking her hand. "It's a pleasure to meet you properly at last. I was wondering if you and your friend would like to join me for coffee. I haven't thanked you properly for saving my life."

Jim said, "I ought to go home and pack. Thanks for the offer though."

"I'd love to," Lou said. "Let me just go and get changed."

"I'll meet you in the cafeteria."

Jim went back up to the house. "I'm back," he said, running up the stairs.

"Did that police officer find you?" Nichola asked.

"Yeah. He and Lou are having coffee."

"What did he want?"

"He was one of the officers Lou saved from that explosion in the docks last year." He glanced around the room. "How's the packing going?"

Nichola surveyed the mass of clothes strewn over the beds. "Slowly."

"Is Jack meeting us at the airport?"

"I hope so. Assuming we ever get packed, that is."

"I'll give you a hand."

****

In the cafeteria Lou drank her coffee slowly, looking at the figure opposite her. His cane leaned against the table beside him. "How much do you remember?" she asked.

"Not much. Which is probably a blessing. I remember a loud bang, then nothing for a bit. Being trapped under the water, panic as I couldn't breathe or move, and you appearing like a dream. Nothing else until the hospital. Three months in there, learning to walk again."

"That I can sympathize with."

DI Sutton smiled at her. "How long were you in hospital for? Did they airlift you there?"

"Not exactly. By the time we were rescued, five months had passed since the attack. I spent six weeks in the infirmary on the airbase."

"Do you remember much about it?"

Lou shuddered slightly. "Everything. I wish I could forget, but I can't. The flashbacks come when I least expect or want them."

DI Sutton said, "If it were me, I wouldn't be in a hurry to get back in the water."

"Swimming is part of my physio. I wasn't given a choice." She put her cup down. "Are you back at work now?"

"Yes. Stuck behind a desk most of the time

unfortunately, but hopefully not for much longer. I don't need the cane all the time now."

"According to Dr. Andrews, I don't need the crutches," Lou said. "I just don't trust the prosthesis totally yet. And I'm not old enough for a cane. No offense."

"None taken. It wasn't my first choice, but my kids get a kick out of doing Dad impressions with it."

She finished her coffee. "Thanks for that. I really ought to go and pack. We fly back tomorrow."

"Where are you living now?"

"Guam. My mum's boyfriend is out there in the Air Force." She stood up. "It was nice to meet you properly at last."

"The pleasure is all mine."

18

As Bill drove them to the airport the following day, it was still raining. "Shan't miss the weather," Lou said.

Staci mumbled something incoherently, scribbling in her notebook.

"You OK, kiddo?" Jim asked.

Staci mumbled in response.

"You won't get a straight answer," Lou told him. "She's had her head buried in that all night. Writing her life story, I think."

Jim nodded. "I got away with calling her kiddo, so I know she isn't listening."

Bill hugged Jim and Staci tightly as he dropped them off. "Be good. See you in a few weeks."

Jim nodded. "I miss you already."

Staci continued to write during the flight, and when she did sleep, she held the book so tightly that Jim couldn't even pry it from her grasp to read it. It was a long, tiring flight, almost twenty hours in total, not including the brief refueling stop.

Lou looked at Jim. "Sleep," she told him. "Or you'll be too tired to even speak to Ailsa, never mind anything else."

Jim shook his head. "I can't sleep on a plane," he insisted.

Lou grinned. "Your funeral," she quipped. "Because by the time we land, you'll have been awake for almost thirty-six hours straight and dead on your feet."

At the airport in Guam, Jack and Ailsa were waiting for the plane. As the others came into the arrivals hall, Jack swept Mum off her feet into a bear hug and kissed her.

Lou looked at the others and grinned. "Yep. He missed her."

Not to be outdone, Ailsa hugged them each in turn. "It's been a long two weeks," she said. "I'm glad you're back."

Jack put Mum down and hugged the others. "Welcome home," he said. "How was England?"

"Wet," Staci said decisively. "Wet and cold. Typical English summer really."

"Be fair, Stace," Lou grinned. "The rain was warm-ish."

Jack took the luggage trolley from Jim. "This is heavy," he said, pushing it. "You guys rob the Bank of England while you were there?"

Jim laughed. "Spent it, more like. It's what comes of going on holiday with a bunch of women," he told him. "They always take too much stuff and buy more while they are there." He broke off with a cry of pain as Lou and Staci hit him.

"That's enough," Mum told them. "Wait until you get indoors."

Jim looked at her in mock shock. "Don't tell them that. I don't want to be hit indoors either."

Back at Jack's place, Mum was surprised to see how tidy it was.

"All Jack's own work," Ailsa said as Jack carried in the last of the cases. "He wanted it looking nice for you."

Jack shut the front door and put the last of the cases in the bedrooms. "That's the lot," he said. He went through to the kitchen and put the kettle on.

Mum wandered through on her way to the laundry with a pile of washing.

Jack grabbed hold of her. "Leave the washing, Nicky," he told her.

Mum looked at him. "There's masses of it."

"Do it tomorrow. You look exhausted."

"I am. It was a long flight."

Lou grinned at them. "Can I give Jack his present now, Mum?"

"Present?" Jack asked. "Yes, you can give me my present now."

Lou grabbed him. "Come on."

Once the presents had been opened and admired and coffee drunk, Mum went upstairs to lie down for a while. Jack looked at Lou. "Can I have a word?" he asked. "Outside."

"Sure." Lou followed him outside onto the back porch. The early-afternoon sun blazed down strongly. She sat by the table and Jack sat next to her. "I need to ask you something," he started awkwardly. "It's kind of difficult to put into words, but..."

"It's Mum, isn't it?" Lou interrupted.

Jack nodded. "I love her, Lou. I have since I first met her. Not having her here for the last two weeks has made me realize just how much I love her. She has turned this house into a home. You all have, but your mom most of all. What I am trying to say here is"—he paused and took a deep breath—"may I marry your mom?"

"You're asking the wrong person. Isn't it Mum you should be asking?"

Jack smiled. "I know it's traditional to ask the father for permission to marry his daughter, but in this case I thought I should ask you. Lou, it's a decision that will affect you as well. For a start, your mom will become my wife. She will move out of the guest room and into my bedroom. She'll take my name and become Mrs. Fitzgerald instead of Mrs. Benson. I hope I'll become the most important thing in her life, after you, and she'll be the center of mine. But I don't want you to think I'm replacing your dad. Robert will always be your father. Nothing can change that or the seventeen years your mom spent with him. I would be honored for you to become my daughter, but if you don't want me as a stepdad or sharing your mom, then I need to know..." His voice trailed off.

Lou smiled at him. "Jack, I would love to have you as my stepdad." She threw her arms around his neck, taking him by surprise. "I couldn't ask for anyone nicer. I owe you my life. Besides, anyone can see how much you and Mum love each other. She glows whenever you are in the room or someone mentions your name. Go for it."

"Thank you. Not a word now, till I've spoken to your mom."

The phone rang a couple of times. Mum answered it and called, "Jack? General Merrick on the phone for you."

"Coming." Jack got up and went inside and took the phone. "Yes, ma'am?" He listened for a few minutes and then said, "Yes, ma'am. I'll bring him in now. Bye." He put the phone down and turned to Jim. "General Merrick wants to see you now. I'll drive you in and then bring you back." He looked over at Nichola. "Don't cook. I'll bring something back with me. You still look tired."

"I'm fine. Don't be too long, otherwise we'll all be asleep."

Jack grinned and he and Jim left.

Staci was still writing in her notebook and mumbling.

Ailsa asked, "What's with Staci?"

"Don't know," Lou replied. "She's been at it for hours. Days even. Still, it takes her mind off food."

****

Jim sat quietly during the drive to the base. He was tired and his eyes kept closing. It may only be 1400 here, but he was still on English time and it was 0500 this morning there. The drive to the base only took twenty-five minutes. He gave in and let his eyes stay shut.

Jim woke with a jump as the car stopped. "Lou," he said.

"It's OK," Jack said. "We've arrived at the base."

"I was dreaming about sharks," Jim said. "I've been having a lot of those recently."

Jack locked the car. "If you want to talk, I'm willing to listen," he said. "Any time."

"I might just take you up on that," Jim said as they went into the main building.

Jack led the way to the general's office. He knocked on the door. "Come in," came the reply. Jack opened the door. He saluted.

General Merrick returned the salute. "Colonel," she said. "Jim, how was your trip?"

"Good. Thank you, ma'am. Tiring though, but it was good to see places again."

"Good. Have a seat, Jim."

General Merrick nodded to Jack. He shut the door and, remaining in the office, stood just in front of the door.

Jim sat down, wondering what he had done.

General Merrick looked at him. "Colonel Fitzgerald told me some time ago of your desire to join the military."

"Yes, ma'am. It's all I ever wanted to do."

"I understand you favor the Navy."

"That was my original choice, yes, but being in charge of a ship isn't all it's cracked up to be."

"I see. So what would you rather do?"

Jim glanced across at Jack. Jack motioned with his hand and tilted his head towards General Merrick. Jim looked at her. "I'd like to join the Air Force."

"The Royal Air Force, I assume?"

"I'd prefer the US Air Force, but I don't suppose that's possible, being British and all."

"Why the US Air Force and not the RAF?"

"I want to give something back. We owe you our lives. Plus which, I've always wanted to be an astronaut, and you can't do that from the Navy."

General Merrick smiled. "There's no guarantees of that from here either." She picked up some papers from her desk. "Do you remember that exam you took two months back?"

"I haven't had the results yet."

"That's because you took it here. The results were sent here. Ninety-eight percent—the best result out of all those who took it. Jim, how would you like to serve in the United States Air Force?"

Jim looked from General Merrick to Jack and back again, amazement and wonder on his face. "For real?"

General Merrick nodded. "Even though you're British by birth, you can enlist as a path to full citizenship."

"What about the entrance exams?"

"You've done the aptitude test," she said, holding up the papers. "Ninety-eight percent. Do you need time to think about it?"

Jim looked at Jack. Surely he was dreaming. "No. I'd like to join please, ma'am."

General Merrick smiled at his enthusiasm. "I'll send a recruiter over tomorrow to get you signed up."

Jim walked on air back to the car. "Woo-hooo," he yelled, punching the air, as soon as they were in the car park. He looked at Jack. "I'm not dreaming, am I?"

Jack pinched him.

Jim rubbed his arm. "I guess I'm not."

Jack grinned. "I guess not. We'll stop off for food on the way home."

"I might just stay in the car," Jim said. "Let you handle that while I text Mum and Dad and tell them."

They arrived back to find the house in darkness.

Jim yawned. "Maybe they are all asleep."

"Maybe," Jack replied.

They walked up to the door and Jack let Jim in first. "Hello?" Jim called.

Suddenly, the lights snapped on.

"Surprise." Party poppers exploded over him. A banner hung from the stairs proclaimed, "Congratulations, Jim."

Jack shut the door with a big grin on his face.

Staci hugged him. "Well done, bro. One day you may really be Captain Kirk."

"Once I'm an American citizen, yes," Jim told her.

She let go and Lou hugged him. Then Ailsa.

Nichola waited until the others had finished before giving him a hug too. "Well done. I'm proud of you."

"Thanks. All this, it's...How did you know?"

"Black ops," Lou grinned. "Plus a spy on the inside. Jack rang from the takeaway."

"Dinner's ready," Jack called. "Come and eat while it's hot."

****

Lou was the last to leave the kitchen once she'd done the dishes. Jack and Mum were sitting on the swing seat. She turned off the kitchen light and looked back towards the window as Jack dropped to one knee. She turned away, not wanting to intrude on their privacy, and headed into the hall and up the stairs to the room she shared with Ailsa.

It seemed everyone's life was finally falling into place. Except hers.

19

The following morning, Jack was up and gone to work before any of the others had surfaced. Mum was still asleep when Lou brought her in some tea.

"Cup of tea," she said.

Mum turned over and pushed up. "Thanks, love. What time is it?"

"Just gone eleven." Lou noticed something sparkle on her mum's left hand and sat as she patted the bed beside her.

"Last night Jack asked me to marry him."

Lou took her hand. The emerald and diamonds sparkled. "It's beautiful." She hugged her. "Congratulations."

"You really are pleased? You don't mind me remarrying?"

Lou let go of her mum and looked at her. "Jack is one of the best and nicest guys around. I've liked him since I first met him. Besides, he asked my permission to marry you first."

"He told me that. I thought he was joking."

"Have you set a date or is it too early?"

"We have one in mind. Jack is sorting leave today. He has already spoken to the chaplain and pre-booked the base chapel. It'll be a proper Air Force wedding."

"He was that sure you'd say yes then?"

"We spoke about it a little before I left for England, but he hadn't asked or anything."

Lou stood up. "I must get dressed."

Mum caught her arm. "Are you sure you're OK with this?"

"Yes. Like I told him last night, I couldn't ask for a nicer stepdad. There is one thing though."

"Anything. What?"

"After the wedding, when you move into Jack's room, can I have your room? It's got a bath and a shower in the en-suite."

Mum laughed. "Of course. Will you do something for me?"

"Anything."

"Will you be my chief bridesmaid?"

Lou flung her arms round her mother's neck. "Of course. I'd love to. Thank you." She let go just as the telephone began to ring.

"Nichola? Jack's on the phone for you," Jim called.

Lou got dressed and then went downstairs.

Mum was down just before her, with a pile of clothes in her arms. "Jack will be home soon," she said. "We need to talk to you all, so don't disappear."

"OK." Jim looked at Lou. "Do you know what's going on?"

"Why should I?" Lou grinned. She'd noticed that her mother had taken off the engagement ring.

Staci left the room, still mumbling and scrawling in the notepad.

"What is she doing?" Lou asked.

"I take it that's a rhetorical question," Jim said. "Or do you really expect me to know?"

Ailsa gathered up her books. "I'm going to study in the den for a bit," she said. "Call me when they want us, will you?"

"Sure. Do you want some help to study?"

"No thanks, Jim. Your idea of help is not what I had in mind."

****

Jack arrived home just before one, having done a twelve-hour shift. Mum went out to meet him, while the others sat round the table in the dining room. Staci was still scribbling in the notepad. Lou sat silently, while Jim and Ailsa tried to guess what was going on. Jack and Mum came in and sat down.

"OK," Jack began. "We've called this family meeting because there are things we need to tell you."

Jim looked at him. "Family meeting?"

Jack looked round the table. "I used the word *family* deliberately. Last night I asked Nicky to marry me." He took her hand, now displaying the ring. "She made me the happiest man alive when she said yes."

"Congratulations," Ailsa said. Jim and Staci added their congratulations too.

Jack smiled at them. "Of course," he continued, "this will affect all of you. Jim lives here, and Staci will be living here whenever Bill and Di are away. Ailsa, you are as much a part of this family as any of us." He winked at her. "I'm guessing wherever Jim goes, you'll go too, but while he's based here, you're welcome to stay as well."

She smiled. "Thank you."

Jack looked at Lou. "I'd like to adopt you. If that's OK?"

Lou grinned. "It's more than OK, Uncle Jack."

"Quit with the uncle." He grinned. "You can take my surname or keep your dad's surname or hyphenate and double barrel them or whatever, I don't mind."

"We've arranged the wedding for September 30," Mum said.

"But Mum and Dad are away; they just left." Jim frowned. "You can't get married without them."

"We're not going to. They'll be here for the wedding. Bill's giving me away. Jack's been doing a lot of plotting and planning without me. It seems he's been taking lessons from you lot in how to be sneaky. And I'd like you girls to be my bridesmaids."

"Yes, please," Staci and Ailsa said together.

Jack looked at Lou. "Are you OK, Lou?" he asked. "You're rather quiet."

"I've got a headache," she replied. "I'm really pleased for you both."

Jim grabbed her hand under the table and squeezed it. He shot her an understanding glance. "She's just lost for words," he said. "She's excited on the inside."

Lou squeezed his hand gratefully. He knew her too well. *It was just a shame—* She broke off. Jim was with Ailsa now and she just had to accept that and move on.

"We need to go dress shopping then," Mum said. "There is a lot to do and very little time to do it in. We'll go now."

Lou pushed slowly to her feet, just the thought of going out making her feel sick. But she'd do this for her mother.

Staci reluctantly left her notebook behind long enough to go shopping that afternoon. They were sworn to secrecy over the color but were all pleased with the dresses they ended up choosing, especially since Lou's was floor length and hid her false leg.

Once they got home, Staci shut herself away with

the notebook again.

Jack took Lou to one side, leaving Mum to make a start on dinner. "Lou, are you really OK with the wedding?" he asked.

Lou looked at him. "I'm fine about it, honestly. I'm just having a bad day, that's all."

Jack looked at her. "The truth."

She sighed. "It's the date you've chosen. September 30 is the day this happened. It'll be the first anniversary of it." She pointed to her leg.

Jack smiled. "Lou, honey. That's one of the reasons we chose it. We know it will be a hard day for you. This will give you something else to remember the day for. If you have a problem with the wedding, please say so now."

"No problem, honest. I'm looking forward to it." She sucked in a deep breath. "Can you see if I can go talk to Dr. Andrews? She offered me some meds a while back to help with the anxiety issues and I think maybe...maybe I should try them."

20

As the day of the wedding grew closer, Lou became more and more withdrawn. She was having a hard time coping, despite the medication and her newfound faith. She had begun to experience panic attacks brought on by the ever-increasing flashbacks.

So far she had managed to keep them secret, but they were getting progressively worse. Little things set them off at first—a smell or turn of phrase. As the anniversary of the shark attack approached, the attacks grew in intensity and frequency, getting to the point where the sound of running water or even rain could trigger a full-blown attack.

She could no longer go swimming and she no longer went out anywhere—except to church—but even that in itself was an ordeal. She was literally sick before they left and after they got back. She had also begun to experience nightmares like she had never done before. She blamed her inability to go out on her headaches. She knew she should get help, but that meant going outside. Besides, she felt she could only confide in Jack and he had more important things on his mind with the wedding coming up.

She'd seen Dr. Andrews a couple of times, but not being able to leave the house kyboshed any attempt at seeing her again before it had even started.

Mum and Jack had decided against having a honeymoon. Instead, they had opted to stay at home with their family. After a long talk with her mum, Lou decided to change her name to Fitzgerald, keeping Benson as a middle name. She'd assume it after the wedding, even though the official papers wouldn't be through for several months yet. And she'd already decided to call Jack Dad after the wedding. That would be her own special present to him.

Mum and Jack had bought her a puppy, a cute golden Labrador they'd called Benjy, but she couldn't bring herself to take him for a walk. Instead, she let one of the others do that, and she just played with him indoors.

The day of the hen/stag parties arrived. The wedding was only two days away and all the arrangements were completed. Both pre-wedding parties were being held at the same restaurant, although at different tables. Ailsa and Staci chatted excitedly while getting changed. Lou sat on her bed, watching them, feeling sick.

Staci looked at her through the mirror. "You're not coming like that, are you?" she asked, brushing her hair. "It's a posh restaurant. They won't let you in wearing jeans."

Lou rose and made a dash for the bathroom. It took longer than usual to control the heaves and shakes. She splashed cold water on her face and slowly opened the bathroom door. She headed into her room, closing the door behind her. A few seconds later, someone knocked on it.

"Come in."

Jack opened the door and crossed over to Lou. "Staci says you're not feeling so good."

"I've got a headache," Lou said shortly.

Jack looked at Ailsa. "Can you give us a minute?"

he asked.

Ailsa nodded and left, shutting the door behind her.

As soon as she had, Jack sat on the bed next to Lou, his eyes full of concern. "What's wrong?" he asked. "You've been looking forward to this evening and planning it for ages."

"I've got a headache. Nothing much I can do about it."

"You've been having way too many headaches recently. You've had to give up swimming and your physio because of them. And you've lost weight where you aren't eating properly. Maybe I should take you to see the doc tomorrow."

Lou pulled a face and leaned back on the pillows. "I'm fine. It'll go. I'll sleep it off."

"Are you sure there is nothing else worrying you?"

Lou looked away. "I'll be fine."

"Is it the wedding?" Jack asked. "Are you having second thoughts?"

"Jack, you're marrying Mum, not me."

"You know what I mean."

Lou smiled at him. "No, I'm not having second thoughts. Now, you guys need to go or you'll be late. Please give Mum my apologies. See you when you get back."

Jack watched her for a minute or two and then left the room, shutting the door behind him.

Lou lay with her eyes closed, listening to the others chatting in the hall and calling goodbyes up the stairs to her. The front door shut and car doors banged. As the car started and pulled away, Lou opened her eyes. She sat up on the bed.

She desperately wanted to go, but just couldn't face going outside. She grabbed her crutches and swung herself across to the wardrobe where her bridesmaid dress hung. She opened the door and looked at it. It was beautiful, but she had lost so much weight, it didn't really fit anymore. Ailsa had carefully added ties to the back of the dress, under the bow, so she could adjust it on the day itself.

As she looked at the dress, the familiar panic rose within her. She'd never make the wedding, she realized as she threw up again. But if she didn't go, her mother and Jack would get the wrong idea. They would assume that she didn't approve and nothing could be further from the truth. She loved Jack as much as she had her father. She was looking forward to him becoming her new dad. The problem wasn't them getting married; the problem was it meant her leaving the house. If it rained, it would trigger an attack. Or she may have one anyway. She couldn't allow that to happen. Everyone would see. Bad enough they'd see her false leg and not her.

She pulled her phone across and rang the base. "Could I speak to Dr. Andrews please?" She got put on hold and eventually someone in the infirmary answered. "Hi," she repeated. "This is Lou Benson. Could I speak to Dr. Andrews please?"

"I'm afraid she's not on duty right now. Would you like to speak to the duty doctor instead?"

Lou sighed. "No. Just tell her I rang."

Benjy jumped onto her bed and curled up next to her.

Lou rubbed his ears. "Glad you're here," she whispered. "You're like Jack. You don't replace the ones who've gone on ahead; you just help us learn to love again."

****

The night before the wedding, Jack slept at the base, so as not to see Mum. Lou as usual didn't sleep much, if at all, and threw up first thing.

Jim caught her as she came out of the bathroom. "Isn't it the bride who's supposed to throw up? Or are you afraid your mum won't turn up and you'll have to marry Jack instead?" he joked. He looked closely at her. "Are you OK? You look dreadful."

"I'm gonna be sick again." She ran back into the bathroom.

Jim waited at a respectable distance until she came out. "Lou," he began.

"Don't tell Mum," she replied. "I've got a headache. That's what's making me sick."

"Are you gonna manage today?"

"I have to." She went into her room and sat on the bed. She began to shake and couldn't stop.

Staci glanced up. "Lou, can I borrow your per— You OK?" she asked.

Lou didn't answer.

Then seemingly the next minute, her mum was there. "What's wrong, darling?" she asked.

Lou shook her head, shaking so much she was unable to reply. This was the last thing she wanted. She was ruining everything.

Mum looked at Ailsa, who'd followed her in. "Ring Jack."

"But you're not supposed to see him."

"Never mind that. Just go ring him and get him here."

Fifteen minutes later, Jack dashed up the stairs. He shooed the others out of the room. "I'll see to her."

Ailsa looked at Jack. "Sorry to drag you back here. Nichola insisted I call you."

"That's OK." He crossed over to the bed and sat next to Lou.

Lou sat on the bed, drenched in sweat. She was still shaking and gasping for breath, tears streaming down her face.

Jack gathered her into his arms, holding her tightly. He spoke calmly, rocking her gently until the shaking stopped and her breathing was no longer coming in ragged gasps. He stroked her hair and held her, still talking softly and calmly until the storm of tears had passed. When it had, he loosened his grip, but not releasing her entirely. He handed her the tissues.

Lou took one. "I'm sorry," she said. "I didn't want to spoil your day."

"You haven't spoilt anything. It's OK, honey. You're safe now. Why didn't you say anything?"

"It isn't always this bad."

"How long has it been going on?"

"A while. It started off with little things, but it has been getting worse. The headaches were the cover story," Lou admitted. "I can't go out in case it rains. I can't even swim because it reminds, reminds...me...of..." She broke off, panic rising within her again.

Jack tightened his grip. "Calm down. Nice deep breaths. That's it."

Lou tried to do as he said.

"You need to talk these things through," Jack told her. "You need to see a counselor. And you do it soon.

Doc Andrews said that one would come here if you'd find it easier to start with. You can't keep it bottled up. Promise me you'll talk to someone."

"I'm not crazy."

"No one said you are. This is a normal reaction to a traumatic event. You just need to talk it through, that's all. It's nothing to be ashamed of."

"Promise?"

"I promise. And it's S.O.P. for any solider returning from a war zone. No one thinks them crazy."

"OK. I'll talk to her."

Jack hugged her. "Good girl."

Jim knocked and stuck his head round the door. "Sorry to interrupt. Only time's getting on. We only have an hour before we have to leave."

"I must go," Jack said, giving Lou a final hug before releasing her. "I have to get changed and meet Ed. Will you be OK now?"

Lou nodded.

"This is that prescription you got but never filled." Jack took a container from his pocket and pressed it into her hand. "One now, one tonight, and then one in the morning. The doc wants to see you soon."

"Thanks, Jack. See you at the church."

Jack stood up. He left, pausing on the landing. "I'm going now, Nicky. It's safe to come out. See you in church. Don't be late."

"I wouldn't dare," came the reply. As the front door slammed shut, Mum came into Lou's room and sat next to her. "Are you OK, love?"

"I think so. Thanks for calling him. I'm sorry, Mum. I didn't want to spoil your day."

"Oh, Lou." Mum hugged her. "You can't keep things bottled up like this. You need to talk to

Clare Revell

someone. And you haven't spoilt anything."

"That's almost word for word what Jack said."

"There you are then. It must be true."

"Here you are," Jim said, handing Lou a glass of water.

Lou took it and swallowed one of the tablets Jack had given her. "Thanks, Jim," she said. She looked at Mum. "Do you want a hand to get into your dress?"

"If you feel up to it, love."

"Course I do. It's your big day. Can't have you late for it, can we?"

As the cars arrived to collect them, Staci put down the notebook. "It's finished," she said triumphantly.

"Good," Jim said. "Perhaps now you can concentrate on us for a change."

"Don't you even want to know what it is?" Staci asked, a hurt expression covering her face.

"Later, kiddo," he said, straightening his tie and putting on his jacket.

Ailsa grinned. "You look very smart, Jim," she said.

"And you look beautiful," he replied.

Ailsa did a twirl. "Thank you," she said, the full skirt billowing around her.

"What about me?" Staci said.

"You look gorgeous too, kiddo."

The lilac satin dresses fell to the floor, with puffed sleeves, bows on the overskirts and at the back, and very full skirts. The necklines were heart-shaped and the necklines, sleeves, and bodices had piping and sequins on them.

A cough from upstairs made them look round. Mum stood at the top of the stairs.

Jim said, "Wow. You look amazing." Her ivory

dress was similar in style to the bridesmaids, with the exception of the overskirt and the addition of long sleeves and a three-foot train. The bodice was also covered in sequins. Her long hair hung in ringlets with a short sequined veil and a simple floral headdress.

Lou held the crutches tightly. Despite the tablets, she felt sick and nervous, but was determined not to show it.

Bill offered Nichola an arm. "Let's go."

21

They arrived at the base chapel five minutes early, to be met by an honor guard of airmen extending from the lych-gate to the church door. The organ was playing and Lou leaned down to arrange Mum's train, balancing on one crutch as she did so. She straightened up and caught hold of both crutches. She nodded to the chaplain and he went inside to tell Jack they had arrived.

The strains of "Olympic Spirit" by John Williams could be heard as the three Air Force trumpeters began to play. Ailsa and Staci set off up the aisle, their lilac dresses complementing the red and yellow flowers in their hair and bouquets. Jim glanced at Lou and she nodded.

Bill looked at Mum. "Ready?" he asked.

"No," Mum replied, smiling nervously. "I'm terrified." She paused for a bit. "I'm ready."

Bill took her arm and led her up the aisle to where Jack and Sergeant Peterson, in dress uniform, waited. As they got halfway there, Jack turned and smiled at her.

Behind them, Lou propped her crutches up against the doorpost and walked up the aisle unaided. Jim stayed close by her side as planned in case she fell. And also as moral support in case she panicked again.

The marriage itself took place. When the chaplain said, "Who gives this woman to be married to this man?" Bill placed Mum's hand into Jack's. They had chosen the traditional vows with Mum promising to obey Jack. (She had told him she had the easy end of the bargain. He had to promise to love her as Christ loved the church, i.e., to die for her. All she had to do was obey him.)

Lou wondered idly if she'd get sixteen husbands too when she got married. Four better, four worse, four richer, four poorer. On reflection, she'd just have eight—the better, richer ones. You could keep the worse and poorer ones.

Mum's voice shook slightly as she reached the *till death do us part* phrase, as memories of Robert flashed through her mind. Jack looked Mum straight in the eyes as he promised to love and to cherish her, in sickness and in health, keeping only unto her as long as they both shall live. The next hymn was one of Mum's favorites—"I Vow to Thee, My Country." She had chosen it deliberately, as through her marriage she had become an American citizen.

The sermon was next, with the chaplain preaching on 1 Corinthians 13. The last hymn was "Love Divine, All Loves Excelling," which both Jack and Mum liked. Lou managed to stand and sit the whole way through the service unaided, which she was quite impressed by. It was only when they went through to sign the register that anyone noticed she didn't have her crutches with her.

Mum's eyes lit up. "Where are your crutches?" she asked.

"They're here somewhere. Wanted to surprise you."

The organ struck up and Mum and Jack walked back down the aisle. Sergeant Peterson offered Lou his arm and they followed, with Staci, Jim, and Ailsa behind them. The bride and groom exited the chapel into the sunshine under an archway of swords. After the photos Lou retrieved her crutches and went over to Dr. Andrews. "Can I come and see you?" she asked.

"Sure, any time."

"Tomorrow? I'll get Jim to drive me over."

"OK, around 1100."

"See you then."

The reception was held in the base mess. The meal was a sit-down hot dinner. When it was time for the speeches, Sergeant Peterson stood up. "I would like to thank you all for coming today," he said. "Jack and I go way back. We first met at the Academy. We have been a lot of places together. Fought together, saved each other's lives several times. Been best man at each other's weddings, twice now for Jack. You could say we've done it all. Jack has had a difficult few years but he has come through it all."

He smiled. "Jack has a terrible sense of humor, no sense of timing. In fact, I don't know what anyone sees in him. But he is a good mate and he's the sort of guy you can rely on in a crisis. He knows what to say, how to say, and when to say it. And then there's his lovely wife, Nicky. What can I say? Beautiful, attractive, good looking, beautiful...did I mention how pretty she is? She can cook..."

He broke off as everyone laughed. "If I wasn't already married perfectly happily to Cathy, with a beautiful daughter of my own, I might just have to fight you for her, mate. I have been asked to thank all the people who did the catering and served us. It was a lovely meal, so please show your appreciation for it."

Applause and cheering resounded round the

room. Sergeant Peterson said, "But I promised I wouldn't go on too long. So I will let Jack speak now."

Jack got up. He took out a huge pad of paper from his pocket and began to read it. "My wife and I..." Rapturous applause drowned him out. "My wife and I," he began, again stopped by cheers and stamping. "My..." he tried again, but once more he was drowned out. He turned to Mum and grinned. "I give up," he said and sat down.

"Speech," someone called.

"I tried," Jack answered.

Sergeant Peterson tapped his glass. "Let the man speak. It may be his last chance to ever get the final word in."

Jack stood again. "My wife and I," he paused, but this time, there was silence. He grinned. "Thank you for coming today to share this occasion with us. My life changed abruptly on a June day last year, when I met a young girl in Cornwall. When I ran in to the same girl again on Grand Turk, I knew it was no coincidence, especially when the papers had just printed the story of three missing teens. I contacted her mother and formed a deep friendship with her. When we discovered traces of the missing children, she came over here and the rest, as they say, is history. Things change, usually when you least expect them to. Happiness lurks around the corner of the darkest tunnel."

He turned to his wife. "Nicky, you have made me the happiest man alive. I thought that I was destined to stay on my own, but here I am now. With a beautiful wife and a daughter that any man would be proud to call his own. Even though the adoption papers haven't come through yet, I can't wait until I can officially call

Lou my daughter. I guess I have Lou to thank the most. If it wasn't for her messing up a simple shopping trip, as she put it, and rolling a whole load of tin cans down the hill at me, I wouldn't be here now. So would you please raise your glasses to the one person responsible for us being here today? Our daughter, Lou."

"Lou," came the response.

"She's also asked to say a few words."

Lou pushed slowly to her feet. "A few words..." She sat down again.

Jack groaned. "Is that it?"

She laughed and stood again. "Sorry, couldn't resist that one. It's usually the father of the bride next," she said. "But hopefully you'll settle for daughter of the bride and groom instead. Not sure I want to take the blame for the fact we are here today. OK, I messed up a simple shopping trip and dropped a whole bag of tinned stuff on Jack's feet. If I hadn't done that, we never would have met Jack and he wouldn't have met my mother and we would all be somewhere else right now. Actually, we'd probably be dead...Or I would be at least."

She paused. "Seriously. It began with Jim leaving to find his parents. Bill and Di were caught up in the Philippines tsunami and when the search for them was called off, Jim went looking for them. Staci and I stowed away and many things went wrong because of that. We learnt the hard way that running away doesn't solve problems. It just creates bigger ones. However, our story has a happy ending. We found Ailsa and we brought together two people who would otherwise never have met. So let's raise our glasses and drink a toast to the bride and groom."

"The bride and groom," came the response.

Lou looked at Jack. "And I just have one more thing to say to you…" She paused for effect, hoping he'd like his wedding present. "Dad…"

Jack's eyes widened in delight and his smile turned into a full grin. "What's that, daughter?"

"You better look after Mum or else."

"Or else what?"

She winked. "I might run away again…"

Jack and Mum burst out laughing.

Lou grinned. "Oh, and Jim wanted the final word. As always."

Jim got to his feet. "We know you said you didn't want a honeymoon, but we decided you should. You need to start your marriage on your own, rather than here with us. We're quite happy to lock ourselves in our rooms if you don't trust us not to run away. Failing that, Mum and Dad will stay until you get back." He paused and reached into his jacket pocket. He handed Jack an envelope. "This is from all of us."

Jack gave it to Mum. "Did you know about this, Nicky?"

"No." She opened the envelope and took out airline tickets. She opened them. "Two-weeks, all-expenses-paid trip to La Palma," she said. "Thank you, but you shouldn't have."

"Yes, we should," Lou said.

Jack smiled. "Thank you. We're not packed though," he said.

Lou grinned. "Yes, you are," she said. "Suitcases are in the car. Change of clothes is in the car as well. We are experts in secrets. Bill said he'll drive you to the airport after the reception."

Mum looked at Bill.

He grinned. "Don't worry about the kids. They

won't even breathe without permission the whole two weeks."

22

First officers' log 30/09 point 23

This is the final entry. Mum and Jack, who shall be known henceforth as Dad, have left for their honeymoon. Bill and Di are staying here with us until they get back. It was either that or we promised to lock ourselves in our rooms and not move. Which wouldn't be much fun. Even if it is safer than going outside.

I'm going to keep my promise and see Dr. Andrews or whatever counselor she wants. Not sure talking about stuff will help, but I said I'd try.

I said I'd put Staci's poem in here and Jack's, sorry, Dad's, long list of verses that he and Jim read to me in the hospital. Both make a fitting end to our story. We've come a long way in the past year and a half.

Running away doesn't solve anything. Nor does ignoring God. It's no good telling God how big the storm is. Tell the storm how big your God is. 'Cause whatever your problem, God's got an answer for it.

Here's Staci's poem. Left as she wrote it, with her comments, lack of punctuation, etc. She called it "Island in the Sun."

There is a little island,
Right out in the sea,
400 miles from Guam,
Or so they're telling me.

There also are three children
Staci, Jim, and Lou,
And we can't forget the dog
That just wouldn't do.

Jim and Staci's parents
Got lost in a tsunami
Jim went to go and find them
The others stowed away.

They all set sail on board Jim's boat
A little one called Avon
And so far away they sailed
Towards their final destination.

Before they'd even left the docks
A police boat exploded.
Lou jumped in and saved three lives
Despite Jim trying to stop her.

They had to stop in Cornwall
More food they had to buy
There Lou met Jack, an American chap
And a very good-looking guy.
(Just don't tell Jack, his head is big enough as it is)

They went to La Palma
Lou's birthday on the way
With party games and chocolate cake
It was a lovely day.

Once they left disaster struck
Staci fell off a chair
She gave a shout, knocked herself out

And got tied to the bed for days.

Meanwhile a hurricane blew up
Erika by name
Mean and nasty, big and strong
She tossed the boat with wind and wave
Broke mast and windows and the deck
Plunged Avon *'neath the waters deep*
Till crew unconscious, boat adrift
An angel did them save.
(And I know that's too many words but tough.)

On Grand Turk, repairs were done
And they saw Jack again —
The American chap and very good-looking guy
By the time the boat was fit to sail
Another month had gone.

Through the Panama Canal
Quite an experience
Pulling ropes to guide the boat
Through locks to the Pacific.
(I know that doesn't rhyme, but I couldn't find one.)

Jim and Lou went fishing
One hot summer's day
Lou got attacked by a shark
And I don't know what to say.

Jim jumped to her rescue
And saved her from the shark
The dog was worried and alarmed
So it began to bark.

Lou was ill for many weeks
And then she changed the course
From the Philippines to Kiribati
She insisted that they go.

Then once again fate stepped in
Lou changed their course again
Jim fell asleep, the autopilot off so
They hit the rocks off Agrihan
Things would never be the same again.

Avon was sinking
Down, down, down
Down to see the fishes
Down below the sea
Down to see King Neptune
Away from you and me.

Goodbye, goodbye to Avon
A final fond farewell
But we shan't forget you
Others we shall tell

Of how you brought us safely
Through wind and wave and storm
Our finest friend the Avon
For almost six months our home.

They made the shore and set up camp
The first night they did spend
Beneath the stars, the dog on guard
As they slept upon the sand.

They found a temple and camped in there

That was a big mistake
The natives took exception to them
Staying there and locked them up.
    (And that doesn't really work either but I defy anyone
to do it better.)

They made a friend, a village girl
She said her name was Ailsa
She set them free, showed them to where
Staying would be safer.

They journeyed on all five of them,
As Ailsa joined them too
In search of the American base
Where help they hoped to find.
(Don't say it—I know.)

The tremors grew in strength and then
The volcano blew its top.
For several days the lava fell
It turned the sky blood-red.

Jim said that we should call it Lou,
She said it was more like him.
But we didn't do either, the jokes wore thin
And we headed back onto the base.

At Christmastime, a forest fire
Put paid to all their plans
They helped a village in the path
Of flames and saved the day.

They stayed there for a week or so
While Lou's leg had a chance to heal

Learnt the language, taught theirs in return
A fair and honest deal.

Then they journeyed on
But dark times did strike
As Deefer Lou's best friend
Gave his life in place of hers.

Deefer, how we miss you
The way you wag your tail and bark
The way you made us as wet as you
Whenever you had a bath
Not that that was often
Unless Jim threw you overboard

We left you above the beach where
You guided us safe to
Our journey's end, the Air Force base
Just below your final resting place.

They called for help
And help did come, an unexpected form
For it was Jack, the American chap
And very good-looking guy.

We were met by our parents
All of them, alive and well
YAY (big smiley face here)
Who grounded us for the rest of our lives
Not yay (big sad face here)

They spent a few days on the base
At Guam, Lou spent six weeks
Things turned out well in the end

ck married Lou's mum
they now live on Guam
house big enough for us all
n Mum and Dad are away.

his is the end of my poem
See, running away doesn't pay
The price is paid by the other folk
You leave behind that day.

We learnt a lot the hard way
But we learnt the lesson well
We shan't be doing that again
No matter what life may bring.

There is a little island
Right out in the sea
400 miles from Guam
Or so they're telling me.

Anyway, on to Jack, Dad's, list of Bible verses.

Romans 5:8 — But God demonstrates His own love for us in this: While we were still sinners, Christ died for us.

1 John 4:10 — This is love: not that we loved God, but that He loved us and sent His Son as an atoning sacrifice for our sins.

Lamentations 3:22–23 — Because of the Lord's great love we are not consumed, for His compassions never fail. They are new every morning; great is Your faithfulness.

Lamentations 3:32–33 — Though He brings grief, He will show compassion, so great is His unfailing love. For He does not willingly bring affliction or grief to anyone.

Isaiah 38:17 — Surely it was for my benefit that I suffered such anguish. In Your love You kept me from the pit of destruction; You have put all my sins behind Your

Matthew 11:28—Come to Me, all you who are *w*and burdened, and I will give you rest.

Acts 2:21—Everyone who calls on the name of the Lor*d*will be saved.

1 Peter 5:7—Cast all your anxiety on Him because He cares for you.

Ephesians 2:4–5—But because of His great love for us, God, who is rich in mercy, made us alive with Christ even when we were dead in transgressions—it is by grace you have been saved.

1 Timothy 1:15—Christ Jesus came into the world to save sinners—of whom I am the worst.

Romans 3:23—For all have sinned and fall short of the glory of God.

Romans 6:23—For the wages of sin is death, but the gift of God is eternal life in Christ Jesus our Lord.

Joel 2:32—And everyone who calls on the name of the Lord will be saved.

Deuteronomy 30:11–20—Now what I am commanding you today is not too difficult for you or beyond your reach. It is not up in heaven, so that you have to ask, "Who will ascend into heaven to get it and proclaim it to us so we may obey it?" Nor is it beyond the sea, so that you have to ask, "Who will cross the sea to get it and proclaim it to us so we may obey it?" No, the word is very near you; it is in your mouth and in your heart so you may obey it.

See, I set before you today life and prosperity, death and destruction. For I command you today to love the Lord your God, to walk in obedience to Him, and to keep His commands, decrees and laws; then you will live and increase, and the Lord your God will bless you in the land you are entering to possess.

But if your heart turns away and you are not obedient,

and if you are drawn away to bow down to other gods and worship them, I declare to you this day that you will certainly be destroyed. You will not live long in the land you are crossing the Jordan to enter and possess.

This day I call the heavens and the earth as witnesses against you that I have set before you life and death, blessings and curses. Now choose life, so that you and your children may live and that you may love the Lord your God, listen to His voice, and hold fast to Him. For the Lord is your life, and He will give you many years in the land He swore to give to your fathers, Abraham, Isaac and Jacob.

Debating how to end this. Do I draw a nice big picture for Jim, a few squiggles, or a big fancy The End, *or...Oh, I know...the perfect way to end a logbook.*

Bye.

Waves.

See ya.

Only kidding.

Gonna end with my fave Bible verse.

Psalm 107:28–30 — Then they cried out to the Lord in their trouble, and He brought them out of their distress. He stilled the storm to a whisper; the waves of the sea were hushed. They were glad when it grew calm, and He guided them to their desired haven.

Bet ya thought I'd gone...Nope.

The End...

Thank you...

for purchasing this Watershed Books title. For other inspirational stories, please visit our on-line bookstore at www.pelicanbookgroup.com.

For questions or more information, contact us at customer@pelicanbookgroup.com.

Watershed Books
Make a Splash!™
an imprint of Pelican Ventures Book Group
www.PelicanBookGroup.com

Connect with Us
www.facebook.com/Pelicanbookgroup
www.twitter.com/pelicanbookgrp

To receive news and specials, subscribe to our bulletin
http://pelink.us/bulletin

May God's glory shine through
this inspirational work of fiction.

AMDG

Free Book Offer

We're looking for booklovers like you to partner with us! Join our team of influencers today and receive at least one free eBook per month. Maybe more!

For more information
Visit http://pelicanbookgroup.com/booklovers
or e-mail
booklovers@pelicanbookgroup.com

www.ingramcontent.com/pod-product-compliance
Lightning Source LLC
Chambersburg PA
CBHW022158240626
47153CB00007B/2719

As Jack married Lou's mum
And they now live on Guam
In a house big enough for us all
When Mum and Dad are away.

So this is the end of my poem
See, running away doesn't pay
The price is paid by the other folk
You leave behind that day.

We learnt a lot the hard way
But we learnt the lesson well
We shan't be doing that again
No matter what life may bring.

There is a little island
Right out in the sea
400 miles from Guam
Or so they're telling me.

Anyway, on to Jack, Dad's, list of Bible verses.

Romans 5:8 — But God demonstrates His own love for us in this: While we were still sinners, Christ died for us.

1 John 4:10 — This is love: not that we loved God, but that He loved us and sent His Son as an atoning sacrifice for our sins.

Lamentations 3:22–23 — Because of the Lord's great love we are not consumed, for His compassions never fail. They are new every morning; great is Your faithfulness.

Lamentations 3:32–33 — Though He brings grief, He will show compassion, so great is His unfailing love. For He does not willingly bring affliction or grief to anyone.

Isaiah 38:17 — Surely it was for my benefit that I suffered such anguish. In Your love You kept me from the pit of destruction; You have put all my sins behind Your back.

Matthew 11:28 — Come to Me, all you who are weary and burdened, and I will give you rest.

Acts 2:21 — Everyone who calls on the name of the Lord will be saved.

1 Peter 5:7 — Cast all your anxiety on Him because He cares for you.

Ephesians 2:4–5 — But because of His great love for us, God, who is rich in mercy, made us alive with Christ even when we were dead in transgressions — it is by grace you have been saved.

1 Timothy 1:15 — Christ Jesus came into the world to save sinners — of whom I am the worst.

Romans 3:23 — For all have sinned and fall short of the glory of God.

Romans 6:23 — For the wages of sin is death, but the gift of God is eternal life in Christ Jesus our Lord.

Joel 2:32 — And everyone who calls on the name of the Lord will be saved.

Deuteronomy 30:11–20 — Now what I am commanding you today is not too difficult for you or beyond your reach. It is not up in heaven, so that you have to ask, "Who will ascend into heaven to get it and proclaim it to us so we may obey it?" Nor is it beyond the sea, so that you have to ask, "Who will cross the sea to get it and proclaim it to us so we may obey it?" No, the word is very near you; it is in your mouth and in your heart so you may obey it.

See, I set before you today life and prosperity, death and destruction. For I command you today to love the Lord your God, to walk in obedience to Him, and to keep His commands, decrees and laws; then you will live and increase, and the Lord your God will bless you in the land you are entering to possess.

But if your heart turns away and you are not obedient,